Gratitude Happens

Heather Martin

Published by Heather Martin, 2024.

This is a work of fiction. Similarities to real people, places, or events are entirely coincidental.

GRATITUDE HAPPENS

First edition. February 14, 2024.

Copyright © 2024 Heather Martin.

ISBN: 979-8223205036

Written by Heather Martin.

To all those women learning to love, honor, and value themselves. You **are** worthy.

Chapter 1: Sage

A 40-year-old divorcée.
The morning after Valentine's Day.
A note from her date.
Chrissie,
I had a great time last night on our date. I'm sorry I had to rush off, but you were sleeping peacefully. My agent booked an early audition for me that I couldn't miss. Let's talk soon. I'll give you a call.
-John

Chrissie smiled as she held the note close to her chest, relishing the memory of her date—and her first sexual encounter since her divorce almost two years earlier. She'd planned to be a good girl and not sleep with John on their first date. Apparently, she had needed intimacy more than she realized. Plus, her daily tarot card on Valentine's Day had been "Bask in Love's Glow," which made her more open to possibilities. And penetration.

Chrissie had seen so many women her age repel Mister Right with their bitterness and bad habits that on her fortieth birthday—following her divorce from Teddy—Chrissie had vowed she would be different. She would dispel every plume of negativity from her auric field so love and wondrous miracles could flow effortlessly into her life.

Granted, such a feat had always been easier said than done, but in the end her patience and trust in the process had been rewarded.

She stretched, feeling the long-overdue relief radiating throughout her body from last night's endeavors. Untangling herself from the mess of sheets and blankets that cozily cocooned her, she sat up and looked around. Pieces of her clothing littered the floor; her panties hung limply from a bedpost like a flag on a windless day. Of course, John had been anything *but* limp when he'd been with her. Giggling to herself, Chrissie closed her eyes and allowed herself to take in a deep breath full of gratitude. She finally sighed, got up and grabbed the robe hanging next to her door, and put it on. *Time to start the day.*

Chrissie made her way to the living room, John's note in hand. She sat down on her orange pleather sofa and gazed outside the window for a moment, wishing to relish her recent adventure a little longer. She read over John's note again, but as she did, past experiences with her ex-husband started to roll through her mind.

Teddy always knew the right thing to say or do. He made her feel loved, hopeful, protected... right up until he just left her in the lurch. It was a vicious cycle: He'd lead her on, then ghost her, only to soon return with copious love-bombing and sincere-sounding yet hollow promises that inevitably led to more abandonment.

Her stomach dropped and her hand tightened around John's note. It was probably his way of letting her down easy. Just like her ex-husband, John was likely ghosting her but didn't want her to feel abandoned right away. She sat up and slammed her fist down on the coffee table in a rage. A vase fell over, knocking her recently purchased healing selenite crystal onto the carpet. *Fuck.* Selenite was *supposed* to repel negativity and enhance judgment—so why did she feel so awful inside?

She picked up the crystal and held it to her chest. *Deep breaths, Chrissie. Deep, healing breaths.* She breathed deeply in and out, hoping to calm the feelings boiling inside her.

Her cell phone pinged. *Maybe that's him?*

She got up from the sofa and raced to the dining table to check her iPhone. It was a voicemail from her mother. Chrissie sighed. *So much for repelling negative energy.*

She laid the selenite down, then sat and stared at her phone for a moment, disappointed that it wasn't John. Why would her mother call her now of all times? They hadn't spoken in months. Her curiosity bested her irritation. She tapped her finger on the table as she dialed her voicemail and listened to the message from her mother, Florence.

"Chrissie, I know we haven't spoken in a while, but I'd like to see if you're available to come over this Sunday. It would have been your dad's sixtieth birthday. Maybe we could find a way to celebrate his life? I'd like to know what you've been up to, you know, catch up..."

Chrissie missed the old days when you could slam a phone down onto its receiver. Doing so made such a satisfying clack. Nowadays, all one could do was *scream.* Her mother had always been selfish, leaving Chrissie to handle everything on her own. Flo had never been there for her unless it benefited herself in some way. And then there was *the incident.* After Chrissie's father died, Flo had just gone and *burned* everything they had of him—taken a flamethrower to his very memory—and then acted like nothing happened ever since. And *now* Mom wanted to connect? *Now* she wanted to celebrate Dad's birthday?

Chrissie didn't have time for her mom's bullshit. She had better things to do, like purge her apartment of negative energy from her date-disguised-as-a-one-night-stand, pronto. She ran into the kitchen and grabbed a well-used bundle of sage. Tossing off her robe, she lit the bundle over the gas stovetop. As the dried leaves began to catch fire, she twirled the sage around her naked body to cleanse herself. Puffs of smoke curled between her legs and under her feet, over her head and around her hands. Chrissie then waved the smoldering herb like a magic wand as she walked around her apartment, commanding the negative energy to leave through the open windows.

The bundle released thick billows of smoke, more so than was typical when Chrissie burned sage. She took that as a strong sign that Spirit was working overtime to release her home and body from negativity.

The cloud swelled and encompassed the living room, engulfing the room with smoke. Chrissie began to cough. She rushed to turn on her ceiling fan when she felt a sudden heat on her skin, near her thigh. She looked down to see a small piece of sage had fallen off the bundle and was clinging to her leg—unfortunately, it was still on fire.

"Dammit!" She raced to the bathroom and practically tore the shower curtain down in her haste to get water flowing out of the tub's nozzle.

Water spilled down her leg, taking with it the errant ember; it sizzled red as it plopped onto the tile floor. Her leg would be fine, but her ego was bruised. The sage, now burnt and soggy, smelled anything *but* cleansing. Chrissie was mortified by the way her morning was going.

Her back up against the bathroom wall, she scorned the empty white spaces that should have showcased family photos, pictures of her with her dad. If only her mother hadn't burned away every remnant of him away during her manic episode. Chrissie stared down at the fizzled-out sage lying in the water between her toes. *Sure hope pyromania doesn't run in the family.*

She shook her head. Why was her mother Flo getting all sentimental now? So what if today would have been Dad's sixtieth birthday? He'd been gone for decades, and they'd never celebrated his life before.

As if she had the time to think about this now. It was already 7:30 a.m., and she had to get ready for work... even if all she really wanted to do was sit down in the puddle and mope. So many memories, so much uncertainty. Why couldn't life be more predictable, like reading a pack of tarot cards?

Chrissie was already running late to work, and the LA traffic didn't help. No time for her typical Starbucks drive-thru run. She'd have to rely on bad office coffee to save her mood.

She dreaded seeing her co-worker, Ray. Yesterday she'd bragged to him about her hot date, showing off a shirtless photo of John. "Be careful with them Match hookups. You know they tryin' to get some," Ray had mumbled. As soon as he saw her, she knew he would ask her about the date. She could see it so clearly in her mind: Ray, glancing at Chrissie from his desk, his expression inquisitive and oozing an "I told you so" vibe.

When she arrived, Chrissie worked hard to ignore Ray's attentive gaze. She marched past him and shoved her purse in the cubby hole, then set her lunch—a prepared quinoa-and-brown-rice veggie bowl with tofu—in the office freezer.

Her clairvoyant healer had clearly pinpointed the problem. Chrissie had been repelling the love she sought with her addiction to lower-vibration foods like gluten, sugar, and red meat. Her desire for love had propelled her to choose wild-caught salmon over fried fish sandwiches, brown rice over white, and vegan desserts instead of ice cream. It was a small sacrifice to achieve her dreams.

Christie blanched as she recalled last night's dinner. She'd been so caught up in the moment that she'd tossed her healer's advice out the window. But so what if she'd eaten spaghetti and meatballs on her date last night? She wouldn't let a one-night stand on Valentine's Day—nor all the gluten in the world—get in the way of finding true love!

As Chrissie grabbed a coffee mug from the cabinet with a grumble, Ray leaned back in his chair and gained a clear view of her from his desk. Pouring the coffee, she had no choice but to subject herself to his heckling.

"Hey girl," said Ray, barely containing his excitement. "Another bean-sprout-and-tofu meal for you? I hope you're avoiding brown rice too. I just read a gnarly article about how it blocks the flow of your sexual chi, especially for women over forty. I'll send you the link." He was interrupted by his desk phone ringing. He gave her an excited side-eye as he answered it and said, "Marcus, Shilling, and Rosenbaum. How may I help you today?"

Adding the final touches to her coffee, Chrissie inwardly cringed and made her way to her desk. Today was just not her day. She also realized she had forgotten to pull her daily tarot card before leaving home.

She took an unsatisfied sip of her lightweight, watered-down coffee—made worse with powdered creamer and generic aspartame sweetener—and began to surf Target's website, hoping to get her juices flowing and bring herself back to a state of balance. She needed at least thirty minutes of "me" time before she could actually focus on working.

As she was scrolling through options for individual Keurig coffee makers, her boss made an impromptu stop by her desk. Vanessa Kriper—whom Chrissie affectionately referred to as The Griper—needed help. With The Griper it was never a request, always a demand—and it seemed like no matter how hard Chrissie tried to do a good job, Vanessa always found something to criticize.

"We're hosting a potential client here tomorrow. I need you to order lunch and prep the conference room early. They'll be here precisely at eight a.m.," Vanessa said.

"Okay," Chrissie replied.

Before she could say anything else, Vanessa cut her off, reciting from a handwritten note. "Order from Panera... Oh great. Panera. Again. God, I wish there were better catering options around here. Anyways, we need boxed lunches for ten people. One vegetarian. I need you to get here an hour early tomorrow to test the presentation on the overhead screen before the client group arrives." She gave Chrissie a curt smile. "Don't be late."

As The Griper walked away, Chrissie noted the time on her computer monitor—it was exactly 11:11 a.m.—and recalled that '1111' was supposed to mean something fabulous related to manifesting. She didn't feel fabulous, but maybe it was a sign anyhow.

She checked her phone. *Still no texts or calls from John. So much for manifesting.* She did have a text from a friend who wanted to meet for happy hour after work, though, and

Chrissie could use a cocktail. Or four. Of course, that would mean tomorrow she'd be at the office bright, early, and hungover for Vanessa's stupid presentation. The mental image made her chuckle. That was enough for her to quickly reply "yes" to her friend's offer. *Might as well enjoy my evening.*

Her computer's chat window pinged. Becky from the accounting department was furiously texting her with the latest office gossip. After telling Chrissie about who might be shagging whom, she asked about her bitch of a boss. Chrissie typed:

Griper wants me to come in early to set up the conference room tomorrow. Doesn't seem confident in me. Not sure why? It isn't like I'm the one who ends up doing all her work for her or anything. Chrissie rolled her eyes. Without her, nothing would ever get done in The Griper's department—much less get done right. *Anyway, I'm headed to happy hour tonight. Wanna join?*

YES! Becky replied.

And so the morning marched on. It was a typical day in the life of Chrissie Demata: shop online, gossip on office chat, procrastinate work, wait for lunchtime, and peek at the clock every so often—but not too frequently, or else time would slow down. Sometimes Chrissie wished her life had meaning and purpose, but she was just one of those people who survived alright churning out the same routine, day after day. At least there was always happy hour to look forward to.

I could really use a glass of pinot noir, she thought as she moved to work on a spreadsheet due by four o'clock. *Or maybe a lemon-drop martini.* Chrissie enjoyed starting off happy hour with a craft cocktail of some sort before moving on to a wine selection.

Her phone dinged. Her mom again, this time via a text: *Wanted to see if you got my voicemail. Let me know about Sunday.* It had been five hours since Flo had left her voicemail. *You'd think she would take a hint.* But taking hints had never been part of her mom's parental skillset; doing so would require empathy she'd never possessed.

A memory of crying over her lost doll when she was little hit Chrissie. Her mom's only response back then? "Quit crying over a doll!" It wasn't just any doll, though. Not to her. She had been really attached to that doll. Her father had given it to her after she'd told him she felt alone sometimes. He had said, "With this doll, you'll always have someone you can play with."

A brunette Cabbage Patch Kid. She had named her Lola. Any time her mother had a manic episode, Chrissie would pull the doll close to her and tell her that everything was going to be okay. Taking care of Lola helped Chrissie feel like *someone* was being taken care of.

And Mom had told her to just *"get over"* losing Lola. That was the first time she understood—even as a child—her mother and her total disregard for Chrissie's dad. Then Flo went beyond "get over it" all the way to "let's pretend his death never happened." Now she wanted to talk about Dad, celebrate him? His death had happened decades ago. All those memories so long ago were suppressed for a reason.

Chrissie deleted Flo's message, then tossed the phone onto her desk in a huff.

She'd spaced out too long and the spreadsheet wouldn't get finished in time, but what difference did that make? Their department was always running late. There was always another day. Chrissie would finish it in the morning.

She glanced at the clock, nodded to herself, and stood. *Time to head home, throw on a cute outfit with some wedges, and get myself to the bar.*

Happy hour couldn't arrive soon enough.

Backstage Bar & Grill was a dark place with plenty of seating, bar eats, and karaoke. Located across the street from Sony Pictures Studios, it was always crowded with the crew—and occasionally, the star actors and actresses—of the latest trending TV show.

When she arrived, Chrissie practically ran for the front door, slowing only long enough to show the bouncer her ID. She'd always found this ritual ridiculous because she was obviously old enough to partake, and the bouncers no longer attempted flattery with comments about how Chrissie looked younger than she actually was. It didn't take long for her to find a seat in the emptier east end of the bar. She hated being crowded by a bunch of drunk people.

First thing's first: Cucumber Gimlet, Chrissie decided, then placed her order.

The bartender—a tawdry redhead named Lacy wearing a skimpy black tank with bright-pink bra straps—delivered her drink. The Cucumber Gimlet always had too much ice crammed inside a much-too-small glass, but nevertheless, Chrissie always ordered it to start her happy hours, even if she had been craving a different drink earlier. It tasted too perfect: slightly tangy, and a bit citrusy, with the softness of cucumber. And it was *strong*. It wasn't her fault she was an Italian gal with an Irish liver who could knock 'em back faster than the bartender could bring 'em out.

As she took a refreshing gulp, Chrissie looked around. The ugly red-leather barstools surrounding the counter were worn but comfortable. Even though the almost-dive bar wasn't anything fancy, many enjoyed coming there for the cheap burgers and alcohol.

Catching her reflection in the mirror across from her, Chrissie adjusted her floral blouse—one of her favorites, as it showed off her bosom and hid the softness of her mid-section. She ran a hand through her soft brown hair, feathering it back. It framed her face, showing off her ice-blue eyes.

She checked her phone. Becky was on her way. Her other friend had gotten stuck at her job and probably wouldn't make it. There were still no texts from John. Sighing, Chrissie accepted her earlier conclusion that she was being ghosted.

In no time at all her drink was down to the last few sips. A lonely slice of cucumber stared up at her from the tumbler. "Is that all you've got, you lush?!" Chrissie berated herself. "You're tougher than this!" She diligently ordered another gimlet from Lacy, ready to quit feeling sorry for herself and move on—or at least drown her feelings under a torrent of alcohol.

Chrissie was on drink number three when Becky arrived. She waved as Becky walked over, her dark-brown, curly hair bouncing with every step. Becky flashed a smile and her hazel eyes twinkled as she sat and ordered a Cosmo.

"We're closing out the end of the month and my manager is getting so high strung," Becky said. "I almost didn't make it out in time for happy hour."

"Tsk-tsk. You're so responsible. I left precisely at four p.m. I have priorities, you know," Chrissie said with a smile.

Becky chortled into her drink. "They get you one way or another, girl. I stay late, you show up early. Remind me: What time do you have to get in tomorrow?"

"Seven-thirty a.m." Chrissie rolled her eyes. "Nothing a glass of water and two ibuprofens can't fix."

The women continued their gossip from earlier that day, Becky dishing out juicy details she had discovered about who was shagging who. Chrissie found herself laughing, enjoying Becky's company and witty sense of humor. A couple more rounds made their way down the hatch in no time at all.

The gin was starting to work its magic. Chrissie finally felt like she was ready for karaoke. Leaving her phone with Becky, she adjusted her skinny jeans as she walked onto the bar's stage to sing her usual song: "I Touch Myself" by the Divinyls. *I know, I know, karaoke is about singing badly*, she thought while adjusting the mic. *But I like songs that require less-demanding lyrics.*

The music started playing. Putting her hands on her hips, she began gyrating and giggling. She didn't know who she was serenading—the stage lights blinded her view of the crowd—but she did feel fully present in the moment. And wasn't that the goal of spiritual enlightenment? To live fully in the moment? As she belted out the lyrics—"*I don't want, anybody else. Oh no, oh no, oh no!*"—Chrissie felt alive.

The song ended. The strumming guitar outro and drum-set backbeat melded with the ringing of generous applause. Chrissie ran back to her seat, her armpits sweaty and her mood flying high. Becky high-fived her for the performance, and they promptly ordered sliders. The gimlets had left her head spinning and she needed some grease to calm her stomach.

Glancing at her phone, Chrissie saw another voicemail from her mother. Boy, did that woman know how to ruin a good time! She wished she could ignore her, but the unnatural number of calls from her mother today had her unnerved.

She bitched to Becky, "I haven't spoken to this woman in ages, and now she's calling me all day?!" She angrily scarfed down a slider. "I swear. I had to be *her* daughter. All I want is some damned peace and quiet."

Becky acquiescently "yessed" her to death as Chrissie continued her tirade. "Well," said Becky as Chrissie took a breath, "maybe your mom really needs to talk?"

Chrissie rolled her eyes. As if it was a *daughter's* job to be there for her mother when she needed it, even though she had so rarely reciprocated the favor growing up.

Chrissie waved a hand in the air. "If I must," she said, scarfing down another cheeseburger slider. Wiping her hands on a napkin, she grabbed her phone and tried to listen to the voicemail over the loud music. The bar was way too loud and she couldn't hear a thing. Excusing herself, Chrissie headed for the door.

Standing in front of Backstage Bar, Chrissie stared without seeing at the gas station across the street. Her mind was all over the place, and the alcohol didn't help. Chrissie shook her head as though to clear it, sighed, and played the voicemail.

"I'm sorry, Chrissie. I know I've been bugging you all day. Look, I don't know how to say this, but they found a lump. I might have breast cancer and I really need to speak with you. I hope you'll call me back."

The call ended, but her mother's words rang in her ears. The gimlets somersaulted in her stomach. She felt queasy, her thoughts tangled. She was angry with her mom, yes. But did Chrissie want her to die of breast cancer? No way.

Chrissie was in a tailspin, her world turned upside-down in the blink of an eye. She didn't want to make amends with her mother. She *wanted* to stay angry and frustrated with her. Flo deserved it, cancer or no cancer. But did embracing that feeling make her just as awful a person as her mom?

Blinking back tears, Chrissie charged back into the bar. She returned to the bar and decided to have one final drink before heading home. While waiting for her glass of pinot grigio, she set her phone alarm ridiculously early to make sure she wouldn't show up late and lose her job. Her alcohol arrived and she tipped it back, drinking long and hard. She kept the party going, eventually dumping herself into an Uber ride home.

Her head rested in the open window. Palm trees and streetlights blurred past. Her soft brown hair was buffeted into a fine frizz by the wind. In a tipsy stupor, Chrissie let her thoughts wander. What was the gauge of a successful life? Was it enjoying yourself, being disciplined, doing what others needed, doing what you needed? Did any of it matter anyway?

One day she was going to die. When that day came, would she smile and believe her life had had a point to it, some grand meaning? Or would she only recall a life that had been wasted away, that ultimately amounted to nothing?

There was a loud and obnoxious noise. Bright light beamed across closed eyelids. Chrissie groaned as she took her pillow and stuffed it over her head, trying to both muffle out her alarm and block out the sun's rays. Drunken sleep was awful.

Drunken-plus-emotionally-distraught sleep, even worse. Unable to stall any longer, she threw off her pillow and pulled herself up, blindly reaching for where the sound was coming from. With eyes still closed, she managed to turn the phone alarm off, then sat in silence for one lovely moment.

Slowly, she began crawling out of bed, moaning during the entire time, not caring if she was being overdramatic. Staggering to the bathroom, Chrissie grabbed the glass next to the sink and filled it with water, then gulped it down in seconds. Her dry mouth relieved, she continued about the business of getting ready for work, brushing her teeth and tongue. She mindlessly watched herself in the mirror. Red, swollen eyes stared back at her; her face was ruddy and gaunt. Chrissie grunted, chugged another glass of water with some painkillers, and jumped into the shower.

The hot water helped ease the tension from her throbbing head. She turned the water off reluctantly, wrapped herself in a towel, and visited her closet. There she grabbed a loose-fitting blue dress she could wrap a belt around for ease and comfort.

Jumping into some flats, Chrissie went to the living room and sat at her coffee table to check her daily tarot. Today's card was "The Chariot" along with the guidance: "...you need to focus completely on the task at hand to become the winner you know you can be." There were a few other words, but that phrase stood out most to Chrissie, who was mentally chastising herself for getting wasted the night before she knew she had to get to work early.

Living in west LA near Culver City, Chrissie knew she needed to get out the door ASAP if she wanted to beat traffic. She gathered up her belongings and left for the elevator of her apartment. As she pressed the first-floor button, the elevator lurched. Her head began to spin. *I should have taken the stairs...*

She swung by a McDonald's drive thru and grabbed a greasy sandwich and orange juice to replenish her fluids. She darted into her usual office parking space at Marcus, Shilling, and Rosenbaum with just minutes to spare. Gazing up at the dull building, Chrissie closed her eyes and laid her head back on the head rest. She needed extra energetic support today and clasped her hands together in a hopeful prayer. Her eyes quickly popped open. She needed something more.

Chrissie rummaged through her backseat to look for her black tourmaline wand. Black tourmaline was widely known to be a powerful healing stone that protected one from negative energies and consequently boosted self-confidence. Time was ticking, and her search grew frantic. She checked the trunk and the glove compartment to no avail. Finally she discovered the poor thing wedged inside the side panel of the passenger door, buried underneath a stack of Taco Bell napkins. With a sigh of relief, Chrissie held the tourmaline wand in her hand and asked for forgiveness. She blew on it and imagined sending reiki—an energy-healing technique everyone in LA knew—to bring out the tourmaline's awesome powers. She didn't stop simply because she'd never signed up for the reiki level 1 course that had been on her to-do list for months.

Completing the ritual, Chrissie placed the tourmaline wand carefully in her cleavage, wedged in the center of her bra's underwire against her sternum. There it would naturally repel harmful frequencies while remaining unseen by her coworkers.

She swiftly marched to the front door and keyed herself in, dumped her purse at her workstation, then headed to the conference room to begin setup. Inside the room, The Griper was waiting and already sporting her infamous evil eye.

"Wow," said Vanessa. "You actually made it. I was just about to call you. Well, you'll need this." She shoved her hand out and accidentally flung a jump drive at Chrissie. It bounced off her bosom perilously close to where the black tourmaline resided. The Griper grunted. "Sorry. That's the jump drive for the presentation. Please test it and check in with me in ten minutes so I know everything here is good to go."

Not even a thank-you for showing early, Chrissie thought. Vanessa stomped off down the hallway so heavy-footed that each footstep rattled the artwork hanging from the walls.

Chrissie rubbed at her bloodshot eyes and turned her attention to the task at hand. She pulled down the overhead screen and inserted the drive into the computer. Clicking on the PowerPoint, the first slide projected onto the screen. She clicked forward and backward through a few slides, then nodded to herself. It looked ready to go. She picked up her cell phone to call Vanessa, but before she could finish dialing, there was the familiar thump of disenchanted feet out in the hallway followed by a rap of knuckles on the open door.

"Finished?" Vanessa asked.

Chrissie improved her posture, attempting to exude confidence. "Yes. I tested the remote. The presentation seems to be working fine." She nodded to the projector screen.

Vanessa glanced up. "Scroll back to the first slide."

Chrissie did so. The slide read, "B2B Selling for Dummies."

"I guess reading's not your thing, huh?"

Chrissie didn't understand the reason for The Griper's comment, but she knew a mean jab when she heard one. She frowned and bit her tongue.

"It's the wrong presentation," The Griper said slowly, as though Chrissie were a child.

"It's your jump drive," Chrissie said defensively.

Vanessa took a sharp breath and rushed over. She motioned for Chrissie to move and took over the computer. Clicking frantically on the screen, it seemed she couldn't find what she was looking for.

She stood up abruptly. "Dammit!" Vanessa pounded on the table. "This is why we get here *early*, so we have plenty of time to troubleshoot before the client gets here. This is your fault for showing up so... so *late-early* today!"

Vanessa stomped down the hall in a fit of rage, her emotion reverberating through the building with every stompy clack of her high heels. She returned to the conference room soon after with a laptop, her face red and her lips pursed. After some time, she pulled up the correct presentation and let out a cathartic groan. She wiggled her fingers absentmindedly at Chrissie. "You can go."

Chrissie pressed her lips together to avoid saying something unpleasant and potentially employment-terminating. She rose from the chair to leave then screeched as something slithered down her leg and plopped onto the floor. Her hand flew to her heart and her cheeks blushed in embarrassment.

Her tourmaline wand was nestled on the low-profile office carpet. Vanessa side-eyed the object with a questioning expression.

I've been through too much lately—I don't need to explain myself, Chrissie thought. She grabbed the wand with authority and walked out of the conference room like nothing out of the ordinary had happened.

She'd done what Vanessa had asked of her. Now she hoped the tourmaline wand would return the favor and give her what she needed—protection from bad vibes.

Without bothering to step inside a bathroom, she shoved the wand back in between her boobs like a sheriff holstering his gun following a firefight.

Chrissie wanted to chill and relax and go with the flow, but it seemed that wasn't in the cards for her. She'd spent her evening on the couch trying—and failing—to stop obsessing over her strained relationship with her abusive boss and especially feeling unsure of how to deal with her mother. Feelings of loneliness and frustration pressed her flat into the couch. Every time she looked at her phone and thought of her mom, something welled up inside of her and stopped her from calling. That inaction in turn led to feelings of guilt.

What kind of daughter would ignore a mother who could very well be on her death bed?

Her inner child spoke up: *The kind of daughter raised by a cold, selfish bitch. That's who.*

Florence. A mother who'd ignored Chrissie when she'd had tonsillitis because she was "simply too exhausted" to care. That day, Flo had given Chrissie two children's Tylenol, turned up the TV volume so that Big Bird's voice filled the living room, then taken a bottle of wine into her bedroom and locked the door. Chrissie remembered how sweaty her face had been, the pain in her throat—and more than anything, how much she'd wished she had a mom who would sit with her on the couch, let her lay her head in her lap and stroke her hair and tell her everything was going to be okay.

Chrissie sipped her third glass of pinot noir wistfully. Her phone rang. Her mother. *Dammit.* Before she could think about it, she swiped to answer—how else would she find the courage to break the spell of silence?

"Hello."

"Chrissie? It's Mom. How are you?" Her voice was sweet and melodic. *Something has to be going on with her. Is she already on meds for the cancer?*

Before Chrissie could answer, Florence rambled, "I had the best day in Santa Monica! I wandered around all day saying hello to all the street people. They are so cool and express themselves so freely! I gave a guy a cigarette and five bucks for a piece of art. It's a lovely watercolor of that town in Italy your dad always talked about. What was the name of it? I can't recall.

"Anyhow, then I had a glass of pinot grigio at an outdoor café and watched all the people waltzing around the promenade. I thought to myself, wouldn't it be just wonderful to go to Italy together, Chrissie? Just you and me. We could meander around a little town with cobblestone streets, eating homemade pasta and wine. And then I got to thinking about Giovanni." Flo broke off her rant and started sobbing for several moments.

Through her tears, she finally continued, "And I just wished he was still around and could see you, the lovely woman you've become. You know, it's *his* fault you and I stopped talking, and I just *curse* the day he left us, and wish we could be a family again." Her sobbing grew louder through the phone's speaker.

Chrissie covered her eyes with a palm and sighed with disappointment. One phone call was all it took to remember all the reasons she didn't have a relationship with her mother. Hearing Mom blame Dad for why they no longer talked? Icing on the cake. Flo never took responsibility for anything.

"What about the cancer, Mom?"

Flo instantly stopped crying. "Cancer?"

"You left me a voicemail saying you might have breast cancer."

"Oh, that. Well. I don't know for sure yet. We found a small lump, and the doctor is checking to see if it's cancer or just a benign mass. And, you know, Chrissie, I knew you wouldn't call me back if there wasn't something wrong. I know you don't like me."

Chrissie didn't like her mom? That was so far from the truth. She fucking *hated* her mother. She also *loved* her. And she knew she would never reconcile those polar opposites. Chrissie had learned to live with the slow burn of resentment, knowing that she could never fully trust Florence.

Chrissie's throat was tight. She cleared it and said, "I hope the lump is benign."

"Thanks, Chrissie. What about Sunday, can you come over?"

She hesitated. "I don't think so. I already have plans." *A lie. Safer than the truth.*

"Well, shit. *Giovanni!*" She called out his name like he was inside her house. "Looks like it's just me and you—and this bottle of Sangiovese—for your birthday. Alright, chica. Talk later. Ciao!" She hung up.

Their first conversation in almost a year. Right on script. Chrissie wiped at her eyes. *Bye, bitch.*

Chapter 2: Memories

It was Sunday, and Chrissie was in desperate need of a pedicure and a mimosa. She met Becky, her BFWD—Best Friends Who Drink—for a bubbly brunch at City Tavern in Culver City. They were both dressed in cute shorts paired with floral tops, and wedges, which they would replace with flip-flops when they went to the nail salon for pedicure time.

They sat at a four-seater table under a shaded patio and watched people pass by.

"What are you ordering?" asked Becky.

"Hmm. The usual. Chorizo hash. Comes with chorizo, chipotle hollandaise, and poached eggs. Oh! And bottomless mimosas," said Chrissie with a wink.

"I'm feeling tequila-esque this morning. I think it's a paloma for me," said Becky.

"Any food for you today, or will it be a boozy, liquid brunch kind of day?"

Becky shrugged. "I'll order some eggs with toast, I guess. My therapist says I need to treat my body better and stop using booze to 'avoid real emotion.'" Becky used air quotes with her fingers and rolled her eyes to indicate what she thought of her therapist's advice.

"Ick, therapy. Reminds me of my mom."

"How's she doing, by the way?"

"Flo fell off her rocker. Again. We rarely talk, but on a recent phone call she sounded like she's having yet another manic episode."

"Fun times. All the more reason for booze."

The girls clinked their glasses—a paloma and a mimosa—together in unison. Alcohol was without a doubt the best method for avoiding emotions Chrissie had found to date. She had just sucked down her third mimosa when their food arrived, and she began devouring her chorizo hash wholesale. It was almost noon and she had yet to eat a thing so far that day. Becky chugged her second paloma and ordered another as she picked at her fried eggs. A small slur to her speech reflected the tequila's effectiveness. The next drink that arrived loosened her tongue further.

"My mom is in Oregon," Becky said, "immersed in her church and avoiding the elephant in the room."

"Is the 'elephant' your dad?"

"Yep. She's divorced and living without him, but never talks about how abusive he was back when they were together or what it took to acknowledge that abuse." Becky grabbed Chrissie's hand and held it tight, staring at her wide-eyed. "How did we survive these mothers who wouldn't talk about anything real?"

"Survive? I'm not sure I survived. The jury's still out on that one." Chrissie chugged another mimosa. This time, instead of orange she opted for grapefruit juice—it was tart and went well with booze, just like Chrissie. She found she really didn't want to talk about moms. She'd rather drink and forget about everything.

"Who needs mothers anyway," Becky said. "All they do is fuck you up and then try to suck the life out of you during your prime!"

Chrissie felt the same about her own mother, but admitting this out loud felt like blasphemy. Good Catholic

Italian girls did not denigrate their mothers, even when such accusations were fueled by the truth… and more than a little alcohol. Despite trying to bite her tongue and hold it in, some thoughts spilled out of her mouth anyway.

"Well, I never really had a mother anyway. At least that's how it has always felt."

Becky patted her arm. "A mentally ill mother and dead father is rough. You'll get over it one day, Chrissie."

Chrissie felt a lump form in her throat as she pushed back tears. Becky didn't mean to be cruel, but Chrissie's reality had been harsh, and she wasn't used to hearing it put so bluntly. She'd had only one physically present parent, her mother, who was emotionally stilted and made worse by serious mental illness. Chrissie had never had someone around who could teach her to process her emotions. On the contrary, she'd learned growing up that her feelings would always be ignored and were therefore unimportant, if not dangerous. Eventually she took the hint and stopped expressing herself. Would she ever "get over it" like Becky claimed she would? She had no idea. At forty years old, she wasn't feeling optimistic.

They moseyed over to the nail salon for their pedicure appointments, switching weirdly between total drunken silence and overly chatty banter. Sensing Chrissie's somber disposition, Becky tried to lighten the mood with fun questions. Had she seen the new girl at work who always wore joggers like they were stylish? Did they think Chrissie's boss The Griper would get a promotion or get fired? Would they ever meet their Prince Charming, a gorgeous man with loads of money, and get to boat along the Riviera instead of having to get up early every day and claw their way through traffic?

They sat on their bums in pleather massage chairs while their pedicurists trimmed and soaked and scraped. Becky leaned her head back against the chair and closed her eyes. Chrissie nervously scrolled through Instagram posts, feeling like she should be worrying about something but uncertain of what exactly. She'd selected a dark-blue color for her nails but began to have second thoughts about her color choice. *Would it look too wintery for the spring? Will it match that new red dress I plan to wear soon for happy hour? If the polish chips, do I have a similar color at home for touchups?*

A torrent of thoughts swam through Chrissie's mind. Relaxation evading her. She worried about anything and everything that bubbled up in her consciousness. The alcohol had only silenced her anxious thoughts for a short while. The moment she returned to semi-sobriety, they made their presence clearly known.

As the service provider massaged her feet, she put her head back and tried to enjoy the moment. The reprieve was short-lived. Her phone rang. The mimosas inhibited her from being cautious about numbers she didn't recognize. She grabbed her phone and answered immediately with a slow, drawn-out, "Hello?"

"May I speak with Chrissie Demata?"

"This is her."

"This is Claire from Northridge Hospital. You're the only person listed on Florence Demata's contact record. She's been admitted to the hospital for a manic breakdown."

Chrissie choked on her emotion. Words meant to exit her mouth got stuck in her throat.

"Ma'am, are you still there? We'd like you to visit so we can discuss her mental health history and medications."

Chrissie coughed and managed to speak in a small, faint voice. "Yes. I'm still here. When do I need to stop by?"

"Today, if possible. Definitely within the next twenty-four hours, so we can make decisions about her care. Has she ever been committed to a mental institution for an extended period?"

Chrissie winced. Every single year—seasonally, like clockwork—her mother had been committed to a mental hospital. It was like an adult sleepover, with little cartons of chocolate milk and outdoor ping-pong. Bindings and hospital restraints were optional perks allotted to those with extreme outbursts. When Chrissie was very young, her father's excellent health benefits had covered the cost. With Flo away, Chrissie would stay at the neighbor's house: the Mewers. They had a daughter her age—as well as an older brother—that she spent her days playing with, allowing Giovanni to go to work and keep the Demata family financially afloat.

If gone unprompted, she would have happily forgotten those memories forever and taken them to her death bed, locked away deep in her subconscious mind.

"Are you there, ma'am?" the hospital worker asked.

"I can stop by tonight sometime. What's the latest I can visit?"

"Please arrive no later than seven-thirty p.m. You can ask for me—Claire—or the attending nurse. Give the front desk your mother's name and they'll admit you to visit the mental health ward."

"Okay." Chrissie hung up abruptly.

Becky was snoring in the chair next to her, oblivious to Chrissie's personal crisis. The delicious chorizo hash had curdled in her stomach, and she didn't feel so well. This was not the way she'd planned to finish her weekend.

After going home to sober up—which involved an uncomfortable nap on the couch with regular interruptions to check her phone and make sure she didn't oversleep—Chrissie was now in her car on the 405 Freeway heading to Northridge Hospital for what would no doubt be an uncomfortable and pointless experience. If there was *any* other family member she could call to take responsibility for her mother, she would have lain a Catholic guilt trip on them in a second if it meant getting them to take Chrissie's place. But no, Aunt Bettie lived in Boston, and Chrissie's father and all his family had either passed away or stayed in Italy and never made acquaintances in California. She was stuck caring for the old broad and absolutely powerless to do anything about it.

She parked in the hospital's garage and remained in her car for several minutes, steeling herself for the task at hand. Her mother had struggled with manic depression for decades. What would Chrissie possibly be able to offer that the doctors hadn't already tried? If the lithium—medication designed to keep her mom "balanced"—was unable to do its job, then what on earth could her daughter do for her?

But what else was she supposed to do? She could have said "hell no" or "wrong person" and hung up the phone, but Chrissie was afraid of coming across as a bad person to a nurse she'd never met by abandoning her mom in the hospital. Why was Chrissie so worried about what other strangers thought about her? Why didn't she have the right to abandon a mother who had abandoned *her* in so many ways throughout her lifetime? Was she a coward because she'd never do what she wanted, only what other people expected her to do?

These thoughts suffocated her brain until she finally got sick of listening to them and suddenly got out of the car just to put a stop to her overthinking. As was so often the case, "fuck it" was the strategy of the day.

She walked through the sliding doors of the hospital's front entrance in a haze, filled out the visitor registration form, and slapped the visitor badge onto her top. Visiting the behavioral health unit on floor three would require all the patience she could muster, else she feared she'd run out screaming like an escaped patient.

Stepping out of the elevator, Chrissie was buzzed into the ward by attending staff. She walked through the hallway stiff-backed, trying to avoid the gazes of other patients. Scattered hair and blank eyes watched television infomercials that blared and filled the bleached, static space with a false sense of normalcy.

Chrissie hated this place. Like, *really fucking hated* this place. Since childhood she had grown to despise everything places like this stood for: the loss of stability, of security, of a loving mother. She had to stop and prop herself up against the wall as she clutched at her racing heart with her palm. Manic depression had led to more heartache than Chrissie could have ever imagined. In the end, she'd lost her compassion. She hated her mother for it.

Two more steps, and there was the dreaded person. Her mother's brunette hair was spiked with a cowlick, and her gaze looked as empty as any other patient in the adjacent hospital cells. They met eyes, and Chrissie wished she could take it all back. There was love, too, that nestled inside her heart.

She took a seat. There was really nothing to do or say. Her mother glanced occasionally in her direction with a twisted smirk on her face. Chrissie wasn't sure whether her mother recognized her. *When she's this sedated, I can never tell*, Chrissie thought. Her mom's wrists and ankles weren't restrained. A good sign.

"Hi, Mom."

"Hey there, Chrissie," Flo beamed.

That took Chrissie aback. Flo seemed like herself, if not a little loopy from the meds. Flo continued, "I'm feeling good, man. They gave me something and I'm just *tasting* rainbow colors and feeling *groovy* in here."

"I... guess that's good. Did the doctor tell you what happens next?"

"Going back to summer camp. Hanging out with all my peeps. Playing ping-pong. Getting daily meds." Her eyes briefly crossed, then went straight again. "You know the drill!"

A nurse entered. "You must be Mrs. Demata's daughter?"

"Yes. I'm Chrissie."

The nurse extended her hand for a handshake, but Chrissie couldn't bring herself to unhinge her crossed arms to respond. The nurse took the slight in stride. Talking to Chrissie without so much as a glance at Flo, she said, "We're going to transfer her to the Sepulveda Health Center. They have an open bed and will accept her Medicare coverage. Your mother needs to be stabilized before she can be released. It could take at least week, maybe two, maybe more. Does she have someone who can care for her when she returns home?"

Chrissie shrugged. *I don't fucking know. She's an adult. Can't she care for herself?*

This time the nurse frowned at Chrissie's silence. "Please consider taking some time to be with her. Even a few days a week can be very helpful for someone recovering from a manic high, as I'm sure you know. She needs someone to watch out for severe bouts of depression, which can be especially dangerous to her well-being. Help during mealtime is a must."

Chrissie nodded slightly. She'd heard the speech a million times. She knew what Mom needed but doubted she had it in her to provide it.

"We'll be transferring your mother to Sepulveda for long-term care tomorrow. We'll have them call you when she's released. They can transport Mrs. Demata directly home with medications and guidance for the next month."

Chrissie pursed her lips. She wasn't going to get into all the reasons she did *not* want to be involved with any of the nurse's suggestions. She did not have to justify herself to this woman at this moment. Yes them to death, then get the hell out was her typical policy and all she planned to do today.

She went out of her way to shake the nurse's hand and said goodbye to Flo. She didn't think her mother would remember the conversation; she was humming to herself and looking more distant than when Chrissie had arrived.

She was feeling claustrophobic. *I need fresh air to breath, pronto.*

Chrissie left the room, but before she could bolt for the hospital exit, the nurse pulled her aside and whispered about the events leading up to her commitment. Her mom had gotten into a verbal fight in a shopping center parking lot then taken off in her car and nearly run over an elderly couple crossing the street. The couple dove out of the way in a near miss. All the more reason that she needed someone to look after her for a few weeks. Chrissie mustered a "thank you for telling me" and continued on her way.

In her car, she felt paralyzed. *What's that thing psychologists talk about? Oh yeah: Fight, flight, or freeze.* She was frozen. She did not want to be put in this position, and she didn't appreciate her mother or the damn hospital trying to force her hand.

Why did she have to be there when her mother needed someone to love and support her? Flo hadn't done that for her. Why did she deserve better than Chrissie got?

Confused and borderline hysterical, Chrissie got out her phone and scrolled through Instagram. There was a healing sound bath and potluck that evening in the nearby neighborhood of Reseda. It started in an hour. She needed something to move the stagnant, angry energy whirling inside of her. Surely this would help? All she needed was to stop at Whole Foods to grab something to bring with her.

Chrissie wished she had a selenite wand with her. At the rate her life was going, she'd need to carry something with her at all times. Maybe she could have a selenite-infused bodysuit crafted so she could repel negativity no matter where she was?

Whole Foods was like a mind fuck in her state. If there was ever a place that said, "you are not healthy enough," this was it. She bought a dozen pastries—six regular and six gluten-free, just in case—along with four kombucha teas. She also picked up chia seeds and an organic red wine to enjoy by herself later on. The total came to $98. She balked. *I need a raise*, she thought to herself. How was she to ever going to afford the half-pound bag of organic chia seeds *and* her regular foods? She could scarcely keep up with the expense of her wine habit as it was.

Back in the car, she shoved a dark-chocolate-filled, gluten-free croissant into her mouth. It was nothing like the pastries and cannoli her family got from the Italian bakery when she was a child, but the warm chocolate melting on her tongue nevertheless satisfied a deep need within her.

She turned off Reseda Boulevard into a little residential neighborhood with plenty of free street parking. She looked in the rearview mirror to check her appearance and was happy she did. She had chocolate coating the corners of her mouth like a little piglet. She wiped her mouth with a tissue and—when she thought no one was looking—dug her fingers into her crotch to pull out a fistful of fabric. Her shorts had been riding all the way up into her root chakra, and removing the fuzz brought palpable relief.

She looked up. Someone was walking across the street. They caught her eye and turned away quickly, pretending they hadn't seen her act of defilement.

Whatever. We've all been there.

Chrissie put on her best *I'm-a-happy-person-because-I'm-attending-this-healing-circle* vibe and exited the car. An ironic gesture, given that she knew only the angriest and most fucked-up people showed up to these things. Why? Because they needed help—*desperately* needed help—and loved to pretend that everything was okay by connecting over "high-vibration stuff."

That was Chrissie in a nutshell. *I desperately need help.*

She yanked the bag filled with Whole Foods snacks from her car, pulled her shoulders back in a more confident posture in hopes of counteracting her self-doubt, then walked up to the porch and rang the doorbell. No one answered. Her anxiety spiked as she waited. Finally, she nudged the door open with a finger and walked in. The home sported an average-sized living room with a typical San Fernando Valley shotgun-style kitchen. Cute, but nothing fancy. Still, it was bigger than Chrissie's apartment on the Westside. The buzz of a crowd scattered throughout the home filled her ears.

Chrissie fumbled to take off her shoes while juggling the snacks in her hands. The host, a woman named Shai that Chrissie had never met, rushed over to grab her bags and flashed a warm smile. Wearing overalls like an adorable Farmer John, Shai's appearance beamed beauty and healing. She was thin and taut and oozed the self-assurance of woman sporting a lean, toned body—the antithesis of Chrissie's own soft and curved one.

Chrissie thanked Shai, then sat down at the kitchen table and nibbled a bite of cheese from the spread, desperate for more energy.

A woman's warm smile turned to ice as she marched up to Chrissie. "We wait until *after* the sound bath to eat."

Chrissie just feigned an ignorant smile and shoved the last bite of cheese into her mouth in an open act of defiance.

Shai's eyes bulged, and she pointedly swiveled away. The woman cupped her hands to her mouth to amplify her voice and shouted, "Hello, welcomed guests! It is time to begin. Let's all get comfy in the living room. Please, make yourselves comfortable on the couch, chairs, and cushions. If you have back problems and need a sturdier seat, just ask."

Once everyone was settled, Shai continued, "I want to set expectations for tonight. This is a safe space for our collective well-being and individual healing. You are free to share whatever you wish, and we all agree to embrace one another as we are, without judgment."

Everyone smiled and nodded. Chrissie watched the crowd. There was a chick with awesome hair—sides shaven and top adorned with a beautifully poised bouffant—who was obviously subverting her own power. Another woman nodded her head constantly, agreeing with everything, which meant she was hiding who she really was. An older woman had body language that suggested she desperately wanted to be positive but in actuality seemed totally and completely beaten down by life's challenges, made obvious by her sad eyes.

Chrissie wondered what others saw when they looked at her.

We're a sad bunch, thought Chrissie. *Coming to the Church of Disappointment with some snacks and all our baggage, ready to unload ourselves on a group of strangers.*

Shai began the grounding meditation. Her voice was soothing as she tapped a cymbal. Its shimmering rhythm slowly relaxed them, ushering them into a trance state.

Chrissie sat down on the floor, surrounded by quartz crystal singing bowls of varying sizes. Shai reminded the group that quartz could transform their energy "if we let it." The bowls rang with different-sounding vibrations meant to break up stubborn, stagnant energy.

"You are guided to sit straight. Shoulders back. Eyes closed. Breathe in deeply. Hold the breath. That's it. One, two, three, four."

The cymbal chimed again.

"Now exhale! Release all that is troubling you. Breathe deeply in and out on counts of four. Visualize that which you wish to release. Form it into an energetic ball in front of you. Allow it to gather itself together in front of your heart chakra so that you may release it. As the chant becomes louder, I want you to speak to this entity! Say all that you have to say to it, then let it go when you feel ready."

Shai sang a haunting melody, then went silent. She ran a wand along a crystal bowl; a crescendo of waves, energy, and sound flowed into the room. Chrissie could feel a tingling sensation throughout her body and then, as a louder sound emanated from the crystal, she felt a heavy weight in her throat chakra, as if a baseball had lodged itself in her throat. She felt at it with her hands for a moment and realized she could not breathe! Gasping for air and choking, she opened her eyes and felt a scream escape her mouth—but it came out quieter than a whisper.

Chrissie could visualize the black pollutant in front of her: a ball of darkness intertwined with her anger, rage, sadness, and disappointment. She watched it hover near her energy field and began to sob. A stranger gently handed Chrissie a few tissues, which she used to snort loudly and dab at the mascara that was invariably running down her sopping face.

Shai softly completed the sound vibrations and started to sing again. The song reminded Chrissie of forgotten childhood moments. Melodies her mother had sung while her father was still alive. Chrissie savored a loving memory of beauty from when she was a tiny child, and her family was still happy. Her father alive, her mother well. She wanted access to that feeling now more than ever. She exhaled deeply.

Shai asked everyone in the group to slowly open their eyes. As they did, she brought each of them a tiny porcelain cup filled with warm jasmine tea and opened the floor so everyone could share what they'd experienced.

Cindy, a mousy-brown-haired woman in the corner, began sobbing as she spoke. Chrissie could barely make out what she was saying, but Cindy's unrestrained emotions made her uncomfortable.

Another woman, Violet, gushed on and on. "You know, this really reminded me that, like, I want to be present, you know? I mean, you can be present, like, doing an activity like tying your shoes... and that's really what I want to take away from this."

Chrissie felt that Violet had pulled her commentary from, like, the self-help book of clichés. She didn't mean to be negative, but the woman's bull reeked of, well, crap.

For the first time in a long while, a smile appeared on Chrissie's lips. Sadly, it was short-lived.

Shai looked straight into Chrissie's eyes, her gaze kind and sincere. "Do you want to share anything, Chrissie?"

Chrissie couldn't believe Shai had remembered her name. Usually, Chrissie went to these things anonymously and left without acknowledgment from another person. She was rarely seen or heard, more a living ghost than anything.

At Shai's invitation, her eyes welled up with tears, and she couldn't speak. She had realized right then that she wanted—more than anything—to be seen, heard, and acknowledged.

Chrissie desperately craved recognition for her emotional experiences, especially from her mother. She'd wanted her mother to hold her and listen to her for as long as she could remember. But Chrissie couldn't verbalize this tangible revelation out loud to a group of strangers. She formed her hands in prayer over her heart and shook her head as though to say, "No, I can't speak."

Shai seemingly understood. She cupped her hands over her heart, closed her eyes for just a moment, and said a loving prayer for Chrissie's healing.

Boy, that was impressive, thought Chrissie. *Shutting down right when you had your golden moment to be sustained by another woman. Look at you go. You can't even do woo-woo stuff right.*

The circle of women slowly dispersed from the living room, but Chrissie remained seated. She felt lonely. She feared leaving the event for the deafening quietude of her apartment. Instead of departing as she normally did after a main event, she instead grabbed a piece of brie and a small mound of vegan bean salad. She nibbled away in ominous silence, nodding falsely as Violet the Bullshitter yapped and yapped away. Fatigued by the exhausting chatter, Chrissie finally caved in and decided to return home.

Before leaving, Chrissie hovered near Shai, waiting her turn to thank her and give her a truly grateful hug. Shai caught her eye and gently paused a conversation to take a moment for Chrissie. Shai's sweetness—and acknowledgement—gave Chrissie hope.

"It will be fine, Chrissie," said Shai, taking her hand. "Tonight, when you get home, it might be helpful to soak in a salt bath and take some time to reflect. Journal, if you can."

They embraced in a gentle hug, only to be disrupted by loud-mouthed Violet. She dashed into the foyer and blurted out, "Yeah, Chrissie, it will be fine! Remember, everything you want is on the other side of fear."

That parrot! If she heard that blithe statement one more damn time, she would just *scream*! Chrissie ignored Violet and smiled at Shai, then barreled towards the door. Like a clock chiming at midnight, the spell cushioning her battered heart broke. Chrissie loudly enunciated every expletive she could think of as she made her way down the street. Inside her car, she screamed loudly. Her primordial caterwauling continued for most of the way home.

After bathing as Shai had recommended, Chrissie snuggled into her robe on the couch and journaled. Everything she wrote down was filled with anger. *Screw my mom for being who she is. Screw my dad for dying. I don't want to help my mom. But it would feel so great to be loved and supported by her.* She imagined her mom cooking pancakes and serving her coffee. Asking how work was going. Offering a cozy bed with a warm blanket and covering Chrissie with it, tucking her in like she was still a child. A kiss on the forehead.

How Chrissie longed to be cared for. To feel safe. Could she spend some time with her mother? Maybe it would heal and nurture the both of them?

Then she remembered the time in fifth grade when her mom left the house for work and forgot to take Chrissie to school. Maybe nurturing was a bit too much to ask from old Florence.

Chrissie was tired of thinking. She grabbed a bottle of Petite Sirah and got on with the only thing in life for which she possessed both expertise and clarity: drinking.

Chrissie got to work late, but there was no boss on-site to berate her. That was lucky. She logged on and went about her business without any interruptions or snide remarks from the peanut gallery. A small miracle.

Then she noticed that an Amazon package had arrived and was waiting beside her desk. She ripped open the packaging eagerly. Inside was a lovely set of Angel Healing tarot cards. She did a quick grounding breath meditation; she visualized a root descending from each of her feet down towards the center of the earth then back up through her root chakra.

She cleared the tarot deck with sage spray, asked a question of the cards, and split it in half. She selected her card and turned it over: Archangel Michael, Miracles of Abundance.

She grew so excited that she almost knocked over her beverage. *That would have been an abundance of coffee on the floor, not Miracles of Abundance,* she chuckled to herself. The intricate print on the card held this insight:

"Archangel Michael is here to guide you as Miracles
    of Abundance make their way to you. Abundance

is not just about money, but also opportunity, love, nurturing, free time, and self-care. Miracles are any unexpected items that flow into your life; things you desired but possibly gave up on, or previously didn't believe you were worthy of. That has all changed now. Archangel Michael says your time has come. Open your arms to embrace the waves of abundance flowing into your life."

Excited by the cascade of possibilities, Chrissie leaned back in her chair, closed her eyes, and stretched out her arms side to side like the famous scene involving Jack from *Titanic*. *I am queen of the world!* she uttered silently, losing herself in the moment. She visualized wishes from her vision board at home, adorned with "successful entrepreneur," "independent woman," and "worthy of love." Unfortunately, she leaned a bit too far back, at which point her fantastical imagination ran headlong with reality—her hands shot out to stop her chair from toppling over entirely, and she strained awkwardly to stay upright. The scrambling motion knocked the cards off her desk, and they dropped beneath her feet.

Chrissie peered around. Ray was nowhere to be scene. Embarrassment averted.

She thought more about the tarot card. It mentioned "love" and "nurturing" and "unexpected items that would flow to her that she previously felt unworthy of." Maybe she'd felt unworthy of her mother's love for so long—resistant to forgiveness—that she could never receive what she wanted from her mother. It was something to ponder before Flo was released from the facility.

Chrissie logged into the IG to see what was happening in the world. Lots of cute puppy dogs competed with photos of cocktails and food—some of her favorite things. A friend had posted a photo of her father with the caption, *Daddy, you are so many reasons. When I was having a tough time last week, you sat on the phone with me for hours as I cried and cried. #PapaBear.* Chrissie hearted the post, but she felt something inside her fuming. Chrissie wanted her own papa bear, a father who soothed her wounds and listened to her when she was down. But she didn't have a father! Her father was *gone.* All that was left was her mother. She was far from perfect, but maybe she really should try to make it work with her.

If she had someone she could really talk to about her life—a coach or a therapist—maybe she wouldn't have to figure life out all by herself. She googled "Therapist West LA" and dozens upon dozens of entries appeared. Yelp reviews. Stars. Tons of noise. How could Chrissie possibly know who the right person was to open up with and share her gaping wounds?

Couldn't she just change her thoughts to happy things, shift her vibration, and be done with it? That's what all the law of attraction peeps said in their social media memes. What if she changed her thoughts to "I'm fully supported in my life's journey. I may not have a father, but I am supported by life in all ways?" If she said that to herself every day for twenty-one days, her mind would reprogram itself. Or so "they" said.

She decided to give it a go. "I'm fully supported in my life's journey," she said, repeating the phrase to herself under her breath. It felt hollow. She knew there was a void inside her, one she didn't look at very often. And dare she be honest with herself—she was *angry* that her father had left her so soon. She blamed him for sticking her with her mom, who was unstable and incapable of taking care of them. Oh, if only she could go back in time and change the course of events. As if she would know how to save her father if given the chance. Even her fantasies were crusted with cynicism and realism.

My anger and frustration will attract more anger and frustration, she thought. *Time to think happy, peaceful thoughts.*

Food. Food was a happy, peaceful thought. Just as she clicked the button to lock her computer and get some eats, Ray tapped her shoulder.

"This must be yours," he snickered as he handed her a tarot card.

The card read: "Seek Help for Tough Situations." The angels were mocking her.

I need to get a fucking therapist.

Chrissie agonized about the idea of a therapist almost as much as she agonized about how she would handle the situation with her mom. Google searches for talk therapy were fruitless. She had friends, but none she wanted to burden with her intimate secrets and tangled emotions.

Instead, she turned to the mecca of self-help: Amazon books. She would pour her entire being into reading book after book. Apparently "daughters without fathers" was a *thing*. Chrissie had become a cliché, but had only now discovered that fact. One book asked if she had challenges with love, relationships with men, and setting boundaries as a result of her fatherless life. It asked, "do you experience overwhelming rejection or feelings of abandonment?"

Ugh, do I. Thinking about her failures and limitations in relationships was unnerving. It made her ask questions of her own, like *is it happy hour yet?*

She finally selected a therapist who seemed to have gentle demeanor. Her name was Cynthia Bhatti, and based on her website photo, she looked kind-natured. Chrissie needed kindness if she was going to open up to a total stranger. Dr. Bhatti also offered tarot and astrology readings, which interested Chrissie way more than talking about her feelings. Chrissie sent Cynthia a quick email asking about sessions and insurance, then prayed to the goddesses that she was on the right path.

She shut her computer and bolted out of the office as quickly as possible to avoid seeing the ogre, Vanessa. She was sick and tired of being abused. It was time for Chrissie to change her approach to life. She wasn't sure how she was going to do that, but she knew she was ready for things to be different.

A bright room, a wooden counter, and a friendly bartender were the only things Chrissie needed to enjoy an evening. At City Tavern Culver City, she ordered an Old Fashioned and sipped it while enjoying the bar's open interior and soaking up the last rays of sun sparkling through the windows. To avoid going broke, she would need to cook at home more often and skip the bars. But the opportunity to feel alive was so tempting. What was another $200 in her savings account anyhow? It wasn't like she would retire from that or grow her nest egg with the miniscule interest rate on her savings account. It was almost as though people like her were meant to be on the hamster wheel: moving fast, sweating anxiously... and getting nowhere. Happy hour made her forget about those things for a while.

She ordered a burger and fries because the comfort food was a necessity. Crispy, salty fries and a decadent bun with melted cheese made her feel better about her life, at least temporarily. She chomped into the burger and savored its umami flavor and texture, and followed up with a little sip of her beverage. It was all so lovely. *Yeah, yeah*, she chided herself. She was supposed to be cleaning up her diet... but every day the thing that made her happy was the thought of a cocktail in one hand and comfort food in the other.

Another Old Fashioned arrived. The crystal tumbler glistened in the fading light. Condensation formed a ring around the outside of the glass and occasionally dripped small solitary raindrops. The large square ice cube melted slowly, cooling and adding a splash of water to the drink over time while maintaining the rich flavor of the bourbon and orange garnish. Chrissie savored moments like these.

Her being started to glisten with the effects of the alcohol and her perspective grew more optimistic.

"How's your day been?" she asked Chad, the bartender.

A dirty blond with chiseled biceps, he had a boyish charm and an inviting smile. He was polishing mugs, and Chrissie found she had trouble redirecting her gaze from his arms to his eyes. "A little bit slow today, but picking up. Hump day can be like that."

"People either need a cocktail to get through it or they get too tired to go out," she laughed.

"Pretty much." He nodded at her and winked. "You need anything else?"

Chrissie blushed. "I'm good for now. Trying to pace myself."

Chad smiled and walked to the other side of the bar to help another customer. She admired his taut buns as he walked away. She turned her chair slightly, opening her gaze to people-watching throughout the restaurant. A group was eating dinner together at the high tops. Two girlfriends were sharing appetizers and martinis at a table. Chrissie was the only woman there by herself tonight. She should have pinged Becky and asked her to join. Now she looked like a sad, middle-aged woman sitting alone at the bar. That smacked of desperation.

But no, Chrissie just didn't want to cook dinner and be at home alone with the TV. She wanted to be around other people and have a good time. But now she was judging herself for her decision to go out alone. Feeling a volatile mix of alcoholic elation and depressing self-judgment, she noticed her empty glass and quickly remedied the situation. Three drinks would be fine. She could handle it.

As she sipped on her last Old Fashioned, she noted that Chad was looking cuter and cuter by the moment. She was gazing off, lost in a naughty fantasy, when a guy plopped down on the seat next to her. He had luscious dark hair and an Australian accent. "Eh mate, I'll have what she's having." The man winked at Chrissie.

Ooh la la! Chrissie's inhibitions were uninhibited, and she liked what she saw. She sipped her drink and grinned back at the man. They made small talk. The Aussie chugged his beverage and ordered another round for the both of them. *Oh boy!* Butterflies formed in Chrissie's stomach. She sucked up the last of her drink to make room for the "freshie," as he called it. They toasted.

Somewhere between a sip and a turn, he planted his lips on hers and shoved his tongue in her mouth.

Chrissie recoiled and screeched, "Get off me!"

The man's demeanor changed in a flash. He raised a hand and pointed a menacing finger at Chrissie. "If you're not available, why are you here alone?"

Chad rushed over. "Hey man, respect the lady."

"Fuck off, mate." The Aussie knocked over the bar napkins and flipped Chad off as he walked out of the restaurant.

"That jerk didn't even pay his tab," said Chad. "Hey, you okay?"

Chrissie covered her mouth to avoid crying and simply nodded. "Can I tab out?" she whispered through her fingers. She paid the bill using her credit card. She'd spent way more than she'd planned.

Hopping into her Uber, she covered her face with a tissue and cried softly in the back of the vehicle. *That guy was right, what's the point of going out by yourself if you aren't looking for someone?* The Aussie had confirmed she appeared exactly as she felt—a sad, lonely woman hoping someone would notice her.

She walked up the stairs to her apartment, and after shutting the door behind her, she collapsed onto the entrance carpet. She sobbed into her hands. *Is this how life is supposed to be? Am I going to be lonely forever, stuck in patterns of seeking a partner to make me feel better, all the while feeling misunderstood and disconnected from the world?* She imagined other people enjoyed genuine connections with those around them, basked in the glow of companionship that didn't have to be romantic, and felt some sort of meaning in their lives.

Not Chrissie. She felt more disconnected than ever. Her attempt to use food and alcohol to infuse her life with more sparkle had backfired. Instead, she felt worse than ever.

She grabbed a pillow from her recliner and placed it under her head as she curled into the fetal position.

Chrissie woke up at four a.m. in the same place she'd gone to sleep and hadn't budged an inch. Her hip was aching from sleeping on the floor. She dragged herself into the bedroom, pulled her phone from her purse, and opened her email app. *Subject: Sick Today*, she wrote, followed by a quick message, then added her boss's email, cc'd human resources, and pressed send. Officially, she was sick. In truth, sick of her life.

She crawled under the covers and went back to sleep.

Mid-morning sun started to creep through her blinds when Chrissie rolled over in her bed, feeling soft and rested. It was a feeling she hadn't experienced in quite a while. A slow morning, with no rush to get anywhere, no aggravating traffic, no need for an interesting and expensive coffee to dull her doldrums.

She checked her email to ensure her boss received her sick-day notice. Vanessa had responded simply—and to Chrissie's surprise, quite compassionately—*Hope you feel better soon.* Chrissie was surprised there was none of The Griper's usual distrust of humanity dripping from the undertones of her words. Probably a safe response since Chrissie had cc'd human resources.

Feeling proud of taking ownership over her day, she wondered what she would do with her time. It had to be something fun. A fuzzy memory of the strange guy she'd run into last night at City Tavern made her cringe, so she decided to start with a grounding meditation and release that abrasive experience.

She sat in her paisley armchair near the window with the lavender orchid and, after stretching her arms, planted both feet on the ground. She visualized a tree root descending down to the Earth's core and then returning back up through her feet. She imagined grass forming around the soles of her feet and grounding earth energy soaring up through her root chakra and throughout her body to the top of her head. She let that energy wash over her for several minutes.

Her mind wandered into the past. Her mom was young, early thirties. She wore a chiffon flared skirt and a button-down blouse with red heels. The outfit was delicate, floral, and feminine, complemented by a mid-length bob of hair that bounced off her shoulders. Her mother was self-assured, confident, stunning.

It was a day at Chrissie's elementary school, back when she was still in private Catholic school—before funds got tight and her parents switched her to the local public school. Her mom had enthusiastically gotten out of the car and instead of picking Chrissie up to get in the car, she'd taken her hand and walked into the school with her. They'd gone straight to the after-school bake sale table. Her mom rummaged through her corduroy purse, found a pen and checkbook, and offered a cut a check in Chrissie's name. Chrissie had been hard at work trying to raise money for the school, and that sum of money on top of her own eager work took her from a respectable rank ten to a boastful rank two on the sales chart for student-raised funds.

It had been a rare shining moment when her mom not only supported her but was strong, powerful, and balanced.

Chrissie's eyes bolted open and she smiled. That had been the first positive memory she'd ever had of her mother being strong and focused—a moment when Chrissie had been proud to say that was *her* mom. She'd beamed with happiness because her mom had done something truly special for her, without Chrissie even having to ask. All she'd mentioned to her mom that day was about not doing as well in the bake-off fundraising competition as she'd have liked. Flo had come galloping to Chrissie's rescue.

She kept her posture and breathed slowly. Maybe there were more instances of positive experiences with her mom that Chrissie had forgotten? Maybe she'd been so focused on her negativity and resentment that she hadn't left space for positive things to arise. She wanted to remember more of her life experiences, instead of getting stuck repeating memories of the moments that hurt her feelings.

She held her hands in prayer and gave thanks for the gift she was given: the gift of new memories. It was time to shower and move on with her day. Brunch was most likely in her near future.

She found herself at Ugo café, sitting outdoors while sipping a cappuccino as she waited for her Bloody Mary to arrive. Despite the horrible experience last night in Culver City, she had returned to the same street. The area offered extensive walkability, and Chrissie wanted to frolic at her whim. Not to mention that a breakfast pizza was always an excellent idea. A Neapolitan-style pizza covered with fresh tomatoes, garlic, mozzarella, fresh herbs, and two cracked eggs arrived at her table, and she dug in. Chrissie wished she could eat like this every day.

Her imagination took over. She was in her own mansion requesting the help to prepare her beverage of choice, all fresh-squeezed juices and fresh herbs. She peered upon her austere courtyard, a feeling of ease washing over her. One thing was certain: she could get used to not working for a living. It was good to be rich.

Even though Chrissie dreamed of being a rich entrepreneur—a member of the successful elite—she wanted even more to feel empowered and valued in her work. Either way, she wasn't sure she had the discipline to pull it off. She didn't even have a decent idea for a business venture. Her greatest skill to date was not rolling her eyes during a team meeting.

Oh well, I manage as it is, Chrissie thought as she took a long suck from the straw in her Bloody Mary. Vodka for breakfast was so underrated.

Between her one-night stand and last night's debacle, Chrissie knew her juju around men was bad. She disliked being aware that her energy was in a crappy place and not knowing how to shift it to where she wanted it to be. Was it because she was still bitter about her divorce? Or too desperate for companionship? Whatever it was, she certainly wasn't attracting the experiences with men she hoped to have.

Having a good-yet-brief relationship with her dad didn't help. All her positive experiences with men came from a time when she couldn't even read or write. Growing up, she'd expected all her relationships would be natural and fulfilling.

Boy, had she been wrong! Dad's departure had left a big void in her heart. And it just kept getting bigger.

She swished the dregs of ice in her drained Bloody Mary. They spun about in a slushy vortex. *Shake it off, Chrissie.*

She didn't want her random day off work to be spent dwelling on negative crap she couldn't change. Paying her bill—after wincing at the total—she walked down the street to the movie theater and decided to watch something inspirational to get her out of her funk.

Respect caught her eye—a biopic about the grand Queen of Soul, Aretha Franklin. Chrissie found her emotions oscillating between energized, joyful, and tearful watching the dramatic story about Aretha's life. She'd had no idea of the harrowing journey she'd gone through, and it resonated with her. Aretha had experienced trauma in so many avenues, like having a child at the young age of twelve. Despite life's challenges, she had managed to become a legend.

Chrissie had trauma, but nothing like Miss Franklin's. And compared to Aretha, she hadn't accomplished a damn thing with her life. She was both inspired and down on herself and her lack of life achievements by the end of the movie.

She walked out of the theater in a daze. The sun was shining bright, and the heat was palpable though not overwhelming. A farmers' market was in full swing nearby, and that gave Chrissie something to focus on besides her mediocre, lonely, unimpressive self.

The booths bustled with color. There were bright blooms of poppies sprinkled with chamomile flowers, dark-green leaves that smelled fresh as spring. Vendors sold chicken satay and barbeque, fresh corn, and other produce. A table filled with sage bundles, candles, and sprays caught her eye.

She sniffed a "Connection" candle that cradled a rose quartz and a small rose bud in its pink-hued wax. It was intended to enhance self-love and connection. It smelled heavenly with hints of florals and the soft trailing scent of vanilla. *I need this.* A "Self-Love" spray also caught her attention, its scent equally mesmerizing and soothing. She grabbed both items eagerly.

Chrissie paid the vendor for the items and took her business card so she could follow her on Instagram. She was pleased with herself. The items would be nice healing tools she could use to support herself at home. *Maybe I should've searched for one called "happy in solitude?" Alas, next time.*

Her shoulders jerked and she swung her head at a sound. She swore she heard her name being called among the crowd of people shopping but didn't see anyone when she looked around. Shrugging, she moved on to the next stall to see what goodies were available.

Someone tapped her on the shoulder.

"Chrissie," said a woman, out of breath. She put her hand on her chest. "Elizabeth. From your church."

Chrissie had to think for a second. When did she go to a church last? Maybe the Agape Spiritual Center last year.

"You and your mom used to visit us in Sherman Oaks," Elizabeth added.

The Catholic church. Florence had spent her time falling in love with unsuspecting priests after Dad died. She'd filled a vial with holy water and gone through the streets of Van Nuys trying to bless people. It was the first time Chrissie knew something was wrong with her mom. She was diagnosed with bipolar disorder later that year.

"Whoa. Hi, Elizabeth. Sorry, it took me a moment to place you."

"That's all right. It's been a while. I think you joined your mom for service a few years ago. How's she doing, anyway?" She gave Chrissie a big, bright smile.

Inwardly, Chrissie was cringing. She didn't want to think about her mom. It seemed she couldn't even escape her while shopping alone.

"She's doing okay. Um, hope all is well with you." Chrissie didn't remember much about Elizabeth except that she wore that look religious people got when they saw potential converts. Maybe it was excitement? That was it. She was a Bible-thumper. She'd always seemed exuberant when they'd arrived together at service.

Chrissie stepped away from Elizabeth to signal her need to move on to more pressing things—like eating a corn dog. Before she could take another step, Elizabeth firmly grabbed her hand.

"Chrissie. We are praying for your mother. We love her for everything she is. Please send her our regards and let her know she is always welcome." She squeezed Chrissie's hand one more time, smiled, and walked away.

Apparently, the church loved her mother. She wondered if they truly knew who she was, or just the pleasant parts.

Chrissie wandered through the stands in a daze. She didn't know what was next, except that she was ready for a drink. *Quelle surprise!* She *had* to have more tricks up her sleeve than simply being an alcoholic. Besides drinking and watching TV, what else could she do with her life? She could read more. Interesting novels with a plot, not more self-help or tarot books. Or maybe she could paint, or start an adult coloring book? She could do those things while drinking wine and watching TV, so she would still recognize herself in the mirror—it would be a gradual, kind transition into better things. Chrissie wanted to change, she wanted her life to grow... but not too much. Familiarity was comfortable. Why mess with that?

She walked slowly to Akasha, where she sat at the bar and ordered a glass of sauvignon blanc. *Sixteen bucks a glass. Shit.* Chrissie's budget was definitely getting blown away today. Good thing she had zero-percent interest on her Discover card until December! She would figure out what to do with the balance later. It wasn't like she was going to get a promotion or come into an inheritance. Managing debt was the best she could hope for, so long as it allowed her to maintain her lifestyle. She sipped the cold liquid and swirled its grapefruit-infused flavors around in her mouth before swallowing.

For a moment, she wondered what Florence was up to. She'd really made an impression on the church's congregation. Chrissie was surprised since her mom didn't usually stand out much, unless she was doing something strange. Wasn't that interesting?

She ordered a chicken sandwich and received a phone call. Answering, she said, "It's Chrissie."

"Hello! This is James from the Sepulveda Health Center. Great news! Your mom is going to be released soon. She needs a ride home from you tomorrow."

He didn't even ask if I'm available or want to help. He just assumed I'm on call.

Chrissie ground her teeth together. "Sorry, I have work tomorrow. Can you provide her a ride home?"

"Yes, we can drive her, but she needs to be released under supervised care."

"That's going to be a challenge for me. Why don't you just keep her at the facility?"

"Oh? Hmm. I don't know. This is an uncommon request. Let me put the manager on the phone with you. Please hold."

Chrissie gritted her teeth and rolled her eyes as elevator music played. Before long, a perky woman's voice spoke. "Hi. This is Suzette."

"Hi. This is Chrissie."

There was an awkward pause as both of them hesitated.

"James said you have questions about Florence Demata's release tomorrow."

"Yeah. I was wondering why... if she needs supervision... why don't you simply keep her at your facility?"

"Well, uh, you see... the insurance only covers a certain number of days. Now that she's stabilized and has her medication, we *have* to send her home. And she needs someone to be with her."

"Like, twenty-four-seven?"

"Well, we can't enforce that... but she does need someone to check in with her daily for the next few months."

"Alright. Please drop her off at her home and I'll stop by."

"Okay. Please meet us at her home in North Hills at four-thirty p.m. tomorrow to sign the release papers."

"*Release papers?* That's not how this usually works. She's an adult. Can't she release herself?"

"No, no! Someone from her family needs to sign her out. That's *policy*."

"What if I was dead, or lived in another state? Then you'd really be screwed," Chrissie hummed softly under her breath.

"I'm sorry. I couldn't hear that."

"Nope, it's nothing. See you tomorrow at her house on Tupper Street in North Hills."

"Yup, that's what's on file. Good. See you there."

Ugh. Chrissie chugged the remainder of her wine and ordered another. Who made these rules? Did they understand Chrissie was trying to develop a life for herself that wasn't tethered to the past? How was she supposed to forge a new path in life if she kept getting sucked into old family drama? There had to be someone else who could handle this. Maybe Medicare would cover a nurse?

A tall, dark-haired man sat down next to her and smiled. She looked and turned away quickly. She was in no mood to think about romance right now. And the last thing she needed was some freak trying to crawl into her personal space. She finished the last bite of her sandwich, depleted her wine, paid her check, and left. Her frolicking day of fun in the sun was over.

Back to reality. Thanks, again, Mom.

It was seven a.m. and Chrissie was already—quite begrudgingly—at her desk. She had clocked in super early in order to leave work early enough to get to the San Fernando Valley in time to "sign off" on her mother—whatever the fuck that meant. She'd sent an email to human resources last night letting them know of her family emergency and that she would be leaving the office early. She'd cc'd her boss too because, *Let's face it, Vanessa is a vindictive bitch*. Chrissie would still work a full eight hours, she just had to sacrifice her sleep and wouldn't take a lunch break.

Her annoyance showed as she pecked at her stale, uninspired microwave lasagna for lunch and sipped on water. It wasn't like she would starve to death, but the food was less than palatable compared to her preferred fare.

As an unintended consequence of arriving early, she found herself focusing on her work without distraction. That day ended up being the first day in a long while she'd finished all her assignments on time. It was also the first time she could ever recall wanting to *stay* at the office—work was far more pleasant than what she was about to do.

It took just five minutes in traffic before she became convinced she would be late. Chrissie drummed her fingers on the steering wheel as her car idled like a sardine in a can. If she didn't make it in time, did she get out of "supervising" Flo?

Traffic scooted along in fits and spurts. She finally turned left onto the Nordhoff exit and drove towards Tupper. When she arrived at her mom's house, she noticed the front shrubs were sparse. Most of the plants were dead. One of the home's address numbers hung haphazardly off the front awning. She glanced at the time and was shocked that she had arrived before the facility van. That meant she had to wait impatiently for them to arrive.

Ten long minutes later, a gray van appeared sporting a magnetic sign that read *MedTransport* on the side. Chrissie's stomach dropped when she truly accepted the reality of what was about to go down. The driver got out and opened the door as Florence exited, donned in all black with flowing pants.

Flo looked right at Chrissie and frowned. "What the hell are you doing here?"

Chrissie didn't know what to say. She guessed the facility's management had thoroughly briefed Florence before sending her home into the arms of her estranged daughter. Why was she being so hostile?

The driver ignored the tension and asked if she was Chrissie Demata. He placed a clipboard of paperwork and a pen in her hands.

"Where's my house key?" Flo said to herself, digging in her pockets.

"I have a key," said Chrissie.

"I don't need *your* key. I have my own." She walked through the side gate and made a commotion as she walked between some plants and a trash can seeking her spare key.

Chrissie was trying to read the paperwork while making sure her mom didn't hurt herself. The fine print contained phrases like, *I agree to be responsible for* and, *I indemnify Sepulveda Health Center* and other nonsense that basically just covered the facility's ass and left Chrissie holding the bag.

She signed everything illegibly and handed the clipboard back to the driver. "Do I get a copy?"

The driver handed her a business card and a stack of papers. "Here's a duplicate copy of the paperwork."

"Great." Chrissie shook her head.

The van peeled off and left Chrissie alone with her mother. Alone. *Frighteningly* alone.

Chrissie plastered on a fake smile and turned towards her mom. "Do you want me to pick up dinner for us?"

Flo waved her off. "I have stuff to eat." Flo grabbed her mailed and scanned the envelopes as she opened her front door. She almost closed it behind her but left it open just a hair. Through the screen door she beckoned at Chrissie. "Come on."

With a gulp, Chrissie walked onto the entryway's beige linoleum floor and observed the orange floral wallpaper that dated back to the 1970s. Nothing here had really changed since Dad had died. Nothing about the décor, anyway. The house had a stale feel to it, like it had forgotten how to breathe.

She had flashes of memory of a time when the home had been vibrant. Giovanni had chased her around the dining room table until she was out of breath. Her mom would show her how to make lasagna from scratch in the kitchen, helping her tiny hands layer all the flat noodles and spread ricotta cheese. She loved pouring a jar of sauce over the top like a volcano erupting.

But now, it was like none of that had happened. Those were all just faded memories. Old and crinkly as the wallpaper. Besides the design being stuck in another era, it was like Flo's home was frozen in time, a sad time. Frozen in the aftermath of tragedy. The closer Chrissie looked about, the more she became convinced that not a thing had been moved after Giovanni's death. The lack of change here held a palpably heavy energy.

Florence used the bathroom while Chrissie looked around. The walls held a few photos of Flo when she was young. One was with Chrissie at a church fair. Chrissie looked like a dork with messy pigtails and a buck tooth. It reminded her how uncool she had been growing up. Despite everything being frozen in time, there were no photos of Dad.

Dad...

She remembered the day it happened, the day photographic memories of Giovanni were removed. One of the worst days of her life. It was a Saturday morning, and she was coloring and playing with her dolls in her bedroom. Subconsciously, she probably knew it was safer and more fun to be alone with the door closed than around Flo, who'd been particularly unhinged at that time. Little Chrissie heard a screaming commotion coming from the living room. The uproar was so compelling that she overcame her fear and rushed out to see what was going on. Boxes and stray individual photos were strewn across the entirety of the living room floor. Some were even scattered over the couch, recliner, and side table. To a child, it looked like a tornado had flown through, picked up all the family photos, and chaotically swirled them around the house in every direction.

Her mother didn't acknowledge her tiny daughter standing in the hallway. She was muttering to herself, clenching and unclenching her fists, gritting her teeth. She had a trash bag in one hand and a fireplace poker in the other; she was using the tool to skewer photos off the floor and place them in the bag. She continued doing so as though she was alone, all the while mumbling something under her breath that Chrissie couldn't comprehend. She stuffed numerous photos—then an entire photo album—into the large black trash bag, tied it up, swung it over her shoulder, and exited through the back sliding-glass door.

There was a large thud at the side of the house where the trash bins were, followed by what sounded like Flo kicking a trash can repeatedly. Then her mom shrieked loudly, followed by soft sobbing.

Chrissie remembered to breathe and returned to her room. She had locked the door behind her and tried to pretend like nothing happened. About a week later she realized that her mother had sorted through every family photo they owned and had thrown out anything that related to Giovanni. Her father was dead, his memory absolutely expunged from the world. Nothing was left of him but her personal recollection. If Chrissie had known what was going on, she would have stolen some pictures of him from the bins before the trashmen came, hidden them somewhere her mother would never find them. Her heart broke when she realized she would never lay eyes on his face again, and she didn't talk to her mother for a week after the incident. She would have starved herself to death if it meant making her mother feel as awful as she did.

Adult Chrissie clutched at her throat. The buried memory was so strong, even after all these decades. No wonder she didn't want to be in the house or near her mother. There was too much history here, saturated with disappointment and sadness. Avoiding it didn't make it go away, but it did allow Chrissie to pretend it had never happened.

She shook her head and came out of her reverie.

Chrissie peered into the pantry. A few boxes of cereal. A container of white rice. An old-school Jiffy Pop container stuffed in the back of a cupboard. She opened the fridge to see a half-consumed yogurt container that had expired months ago. A reeking carton of eggs. An open and undoubtedly stale can of Diet Coke. Wilting lettuce in the cooler. And something in a Tupperware that looked rancid and otherworldly. What had her mother been eating the past few months? Had she been eating at all?

Chrissie started to make a list of needed grocery items on her phone. She couldn't leave the house like this. At the very least, Flo should have some snacks in the pantry, frozen foods she could microwave, and items in the refrigerator not yet past their expiration.

Chrissie moved on to the laundry room. Stuff was piled high next to the machines and overflowing out of a nearby laundry bin. The air in the room smelled of old body odor laced with perfume. Chrissie began sorting the items into two piles: dark items and light items. When she was done, she realized there were months' worth of clothes there, an entire walk-in closet's worth. She stuffed the first load of dark items into the washer and ran them on cold.

She moved down the hallway and hesitantly opened the door to her old childhood room. It looked very similar to how she remembered it. The bed was made with a purple, floral-pattern bedspread she'd selected with great enthusiasm as a teenager. Childhood dolls lined a shelf along the far wall. A small dresser, refinished in antique white paint, sat untouched with several bottles of nail polish and lipstick adorning its mirror. Faded posters of the Backstreet Boys were pinned to the wall. Chrissie sat down on the bed and took it all in.

She recalled reading Nancy Drew books in her corner bean bag chair. Reading became a great way to escape the chaos and disappointment of her life. Why had she stopped as an adult? She had developed her bedroom into a safe bubble where she could have fun, listen to music, and explore worlds beyond her own. She remembered feeling so creative. Whatever had happened to that inspired young girl who made up dance moves and wrote poems?

She left her old bedroom and softly shut the door.

The house is so quiet. I wonder where Flo is.

She peeked into all the bedrooms and the living room and didn't find her. The house was starkly silent. She arrived at the main bathroom. The door was closed. She took her chances and slowly opened it. Flo was crouched in the fetal position on a plush rug, snoring like a baby.

Her mom was safe and sound, so Chrissie decided to let her sleep. She'd take a moment to run to the local Albertsons market and buy groceries, then drop them off before heading home for the evening. But before going, she lingered in the bathroom. Watching her mom sleep was the most peaceful moment she'd had with her in forever.

Albertsons wasn't very crowded. Chrissie imagined most people had better things to do with their Friday evening. She grabbed a rotisserie chicken with a side of mashed potatoes and grilled veggies, just in case Flo wanted a warm meal if she woke later that night. She bought several frozen microwaveable meals, healthy pita chips, hummus, baby carrots, yogurt, and fresh fruit. She threw sourdough bread, Earth Balance margarine spread, and a bottle of cabernet sauvignon into the cart. Flo wasn't supposed to drink wine given the meds she was on, but Chrissie figured a glass of red couldn't possibly make things worse than they already were.

At the checkout line, the cashier placed everything into paper bags. The total came to eighty bucks. Chrissie balked.

She didn't spend that much on groceries for herself most of the time, wine budget excluded. She debated putting some items back, but the majority of them wouldn't expire for a while, so she relented. Hopefully her mother would get some use out of them. And as frustrated as she was with this weird mandate to keep an eye on her mother, she did hope that Flo would eat something tonight.

When she returned to Flo's house, she let herself in with the extra house key she'd had for ages. She found her mother in the kitchen making strawberry Jell-O. She was humming a lullaby to herself as she poured hot water into the bowl and mixed the powder in with a whisk.

"Hi, Chrissie," she said softly without looking up.

"Hi." Chrissie placed the bags on the counter. "I got you some groceries. And a chicken you can eat for dinner tonight."

Flo looked at the groceries and said, "Thanks, honey." She met eyes with Chrissie and smiled broadly. That almost reminded Chrissie of the old, vibrant Flo. "I might just eat Jell-O tonight, but it's good to have options, isn't it?"

Chrissie put the food away and left the bottle of wine on the kitchen counter. "Well... I guess I'm going to go home now."

"Okay, Chrissie. Thanks for stopping by."

"I'll stop by Sunday to check on you."

"No need for that. I'll be fine," said Flo.

"The facility made me sign the paper that I would check on you, so I'll be checking on you regardless. And please, don't forget to take your pills." She motioned to the bottle of lithium.

"'K. Just come after four p.m. I like to mingle with the street people in Santa Monica on Sunday afternoons. It's like my church."

Chrissie nodded. Her mother seemed to be jumping back into her routine easily enough. Jell-O for dinner was odd, but explained the state of her refrigerator. Besides her Sunday schedule, Chrissie wondered what other things her mom did with all her free time. She was collecting social security, though not quite retired. She hadn't worked full time in years. Without a stabilizing medication, it was too difficult for her to keep a regular job.

"That reminds me," Chrissie said. "I saw your friend Elizabeth from 'real' church this week. She said to tell you hi."

Flo scratched her head. "Elizabeth? I'm not sure I remember her."

"She remembers you. She said the church is praying for you."

"Okay then. Alright, honey. Drive safe. See you Sunday."

"See ya."

As she drove home, she wondered if she was doing anything worthwhile for Flo. Something inside her felt sentimental. It was nice to have a mom. For so many years she had wished to have her mom close by and to feel her love. Today, it almost felt like she'd achieved that. Maybe she needed her mom around more than she wanted to admit. Maybe the Sepulveda Health Center was doing her a favor by forcing her to look over Flo.

Regardless, Chrissie would do her best to help her mom recover and stabilize. In return, she prayed she would receive the love she craved so badly.

It was the weekend, but Chrissie didn't feel her usual sense of freedom. The task of babysitting her mother loomed in the back of her brain. Tomorrow was Sunday, and visiting Flo would be easy—there was less traffic than the weekdays and no work to think about until Monday. Unfortunately, a visit to the valley would cut into her brunch time and typical post-mimosa nap. *Whatever*, Chrissie thought. She had told herself she was going to do something different with her time anyway. She couldn't spend her life sitting at a bar. Well, she could... but there had to be *something* else out there that fed her soul.

Maybe a walk or a hike? She didn't feel like driving to Malibu or Runyon Canyon. Even though those locations really weren't that far, getting to them felt like a chore. She did a search on her phone and realized she'd forgotten about the Baldwin Hills Scenic Overlook. It was right in Culver City, with plenty of parking, an easy-to-access trail, and a steep outdoor staircase. That would work.

A quick stop into C&M café for an iced latte and a breakfast sandwich and she was on her way. Chrissie was proud of herself. It was noon and she hadn't had any alcoholic beverages yet. *Maybe there's hope for me after all*, she chuckled.

In no time at all she was at the base of the overlook. She parked her car in the lot and got out to stretch. Touching her toes was a struggle—her hips and neck didn't seem to want to work with each other. *At least I can reach my ankles*, she thought. She sighed and headed up the trail.

The weather was hot but bearable. She took in the sight of wild plants that lined the wooded boardwalk nestled along on the hillside. Blocks away, far below, she could see her neighborhood.

She passed the ball fields and walked up a small flight of stairs. Kids were playing softball with their parents. Couples sat on blankets with their puppies nearby.

This is how the other half lives, huh? The people who have lives, family, connections.

Chrissie vicariously reveled in their joy. She wished she could join them, but for now she'd have to be content watching their perfect little worlds from the outside. Sunglasses helped to hide her ogling.

She arrived at the midpoint of the outdoor steps and looked up. There were probably four hundred more feet to go to arrive at the top. Chrissie took a deep breath and steeled herself against the task ahead. The high steps required her to almost lunge upward, a move her hamstrings were not happy about. *Speaking of, when was the last time I exercised?* She seriously couldn't remember, and there was not enough oxygen heading to her brain at the moment to search her memory further. She arrived at a landing and stood at the side of the dirt trail to catch her breath.

She imagined she looked old, red, and sweaty. Haggard. She watched ladies in fitted watercolor bike shorts and adorable sports bras bounce past her without so much as a huff. *Oh, to be one of the cool girls, for whom life happens so easily.* Chrissie was wearing an old pair of black nylon shorts with deep pockets paired with a Tito's Vodka t-shirt. She was super uncool.

She glanced at the remaining steps and sighed again. She'd gotten this far—might as well go the rest of the way. "I didn't come this far to only come this far," she mumbled under her breath and laughed. Step by step she ascended and finally, her hair sweat-drenched and her t-shirt tussled, she made it to the top of the stairs.

The view was beautiful. She could see all of Los Angeles spread out across the valley below. There was a man-made rainbow hovering above Sony Pictures Studios. Chrissie felt awed and weirdly sentimental. Had it been so long since she'd done something worthwhile for herself, something meaningful? A thing not rooted in avoidance or distraction through food, booze, or entertainment? She took a deep breath and savored the good she'd done for herself. Not just for her body—which she was sure would be sore even though she'd barely walked a mile or two—but also her being. Chrissie was happy to be there in the moment, totally sober. It felt good.

Chapter 3: Sage

She woke in the middle of the night with a muscle spasm in her calf. Sitting up in anguish, her toes curled like wilted flower petals. *I'm out of shape and probably dehydrated*, she thought in a dreamy haze, grimacing from the pain. Polishing off a bottle of rosé that evening likely hadn't helped her case. All she could do was hold her leg and breathe, wait it out. When the spasm finally subsided, she gulped from the glass of water by her bedside.

It was four a.m. She was awake now and decided to check her phone. Chrissie wondered, *What did people do with their lives in the days before a phone became a constant distraction?* She could barely remember the time before her smartphone. She took her phone out of airplane mode. As it connected to Wi-Fi, she noticed a text message from Flo.

There were no words in the text, just two photos. One was a dimly lit photo of what appeared to be the night sky. The other, an image of a sleeping bag on a concrete sidewalk. *What the heck?* There weren't enough details for Chrissie to know if this was at Flo's home or somewhere else. Why had she sent her these pictures? Chrissie was thoroughly confused and would bet money her mom had forgotten to take her pills.

It didn't make sense to rush over the hill to check on her. She would visit tomorrow morning. Chrissie kept scrolling Instagram until she fell back to sleep with the phone in her hand.

She woke with a sense of obligation. Fuzzy-headed, at first she couldn't remember why until she looked at her phone and saw the pictures from her mom. *Sheesh, being responsible for another human being is a lot of work.* It was one of the reasons Chrissie didn't want kids. She wasn't sure she even knew how to help her mom. She wasn't a nurse, didn't live with her, and couldn't force her to swallow pills like clockwork. It was like a weird twist of fate that the Universe had assigned her this duty.

Twenty minutes later she had a giant Double-Double in one hand—surrounded by a wad of napkins to keep the secret sauce from spilling in her lap—and her steering wheel in the other. Eating while driving took a lot of focus. Periodically, she sipped her chocolate milkshake and grabbed a few fries to snack on. It was utterly satisfying, and her car only drifted out of its lane just a little.

Eating in the car turned out to be a great life hack. She didn't even notice the traffic around her as she munched on her food. She felt quite jolly as she arrived at Flo's house and parked in the street. As she got out, she caught herself singing the In-N-Out theme song.

Chrissie took out her house key to open the front door, but the lock seemed jammed. She inspected the key, wiped it on her jean shorts, and tried again. It still didn't work. *Damn thing is busted!* She knocked on the door and waited a few minutes. Her mom didn't answer.

Peeking into the kitchen window, she couldn't tell if Flo was home or not. Her mom typically parked her car in the garage, so Chrissie wouldn't be able to see it even if she was there. Had Flo disobeyed orders to wait for the doctor's approval and gone off driving somewhere? At that thought, Chrissie's happy mood took a bit of a dent. Finagling with a door handle in the scouring heat was no fun. Her stomach jumped and her nerves tingled as her anxiety rose.

She walked through the side gate around to the back. In her experience, the sliding glass door there was pretty much always unlocked. *Voilà!* She was inside.

Now what? Chrissie called out, "Flo, are you here?" There was no response. She muttered to herself, "I don't know where she would have gone…"

She walked through the house and checked every room. It appeared Florence had pulled a disappearing act. That concerned Chrissie. Where had she gone? *Maybe she's at the neighbor's house.* Chrissie had known the Smiths since childhood, so she decided to go ask them.

She exited the front door, closing it behind her without locking it. She walked out of the house, across the lawn, and knocked on the Smiths' yellow door.

"Chrissie?" said Anne, opening the door. "Is that you? Oh, it is! It's nice to see you."

Chrissie smiled. "Hi, Anne, I hope all is well. I'm here visiting my mom… well, under her doctor's advisement… and she doesn't appear to be home. She's not supposed to go out, and I just don't know where she would be."

"I wish I could help. It's been a long time since we've seen you," Anne said, furrowing her brow. "Your mom has been a bit unstable lately. I know she's struggled for a long time, but recently she's seemed even more distant. She rarely waves at me, even when I'm in the front yard watering the rose bushes. I worry about her, you know. It's a good thing you started visiting her again. She really needs family at a time like this."

So her neighbor had no helpful clues, just a chastising speech. That wasn't helpful. Despite herself, Chrissie gave an obligatory smile and kept pressing. "Any idea where she spends her time these days?"

"I wish I could tell you, darling. Unfortunately, we've grown apart these past few years. Why don't you leave me your phone number? I can call you if I see her."

"Sure."

Anne shut the door slightly and returned a minute later with a notepad and a pen.

Chrissie wrote down her cell phone number and handed it back to her. "Thank you," she said, trying to express genuine appreciation. Being in touch with a neighbor could only help her cause.

Anne smiled and closed the door.

Back to Flo's house. Chrissie wasn't sure what to do. She went inside and plopped down on the couch. She riffled through a stack of magazines and found a *People* magazine from last year. Perusing it, she found a piece of mail stashed in between one of the pages. It was an electric bill. She went to put it on the coffee table and noticed the envelope had a red past-due stamp. Was her mom having trouble paying the bills? She'd always made it seem like her dad's life insurance and social security were plenty to live off of. Maybe she'd just forgotten to pay a bill on time?

Being emotionally estranged from a family member was weird. Chrissie thought, *You grow up with them your whole life, live in the same house, and then decades later you feel like you're supposed to know more about them than anyone else. Yet somehow, you didn't know anything. What medications were they on, and what doses at what time each day? When did they eat their meals? Who, if anyone, did they spend their time with each day? What was their favorite pastime?*

Her mother was a stranger to her, just like anyone she passed on the street. She'd given birth to Chrissie, but it turned out she was just another human being with nuances and secrets and tendencies. At one time in her life Chrissie had fantasized that her mother was supposed to be her very best friend. That illusion had long since shattered.

She rested her head on her hand and started to nod off.

When she awoke in the afternoon, Chrissie heard Flo rummaging around the back patio and went out to see her.

"What are you doing here?" she asked Chrissie.

"Where have you been?"

"None of your business."

"I came to visit, like I said."

"You don't need to check on me! I can take care of myself."

"The empty fridge last week and a past-due electric bill I found earlier suggest otherwise." Her mom stared at her, tongue-tied. Chrissie didn't know when she'd gotten so bossy. She continued, "Besides, I'm here because your attending physician asked me to take care of you. I'm the only one you've got."

Flo gave her a bit of side-eye. She was wearing a black halter top and a flowing floral black-and-white print skirt with flip-flops.

Chrissie looked her up and down. "You look very beachy. Where were you, anyway?"

"If you must know, I had a very exhilarating field trip and spent the night at Venice Beach."

"That doesn't sound very safe," Chrissie retorted.

"Nothing's safe in life, dear. I remember I used to think everything was under my control. I couldn't have been more wrong! Now when I want an adventure, I like to get up and go without hesitation, come what be. Why worry? Lord knows there's enough that can happen beyond our control."

Her mom sounded very wise-minded, if not a bit cynical.

"I'm just here to make sure you're taking your medication and eating your meals."

"I'm not a child. When I'm hungry, I'll eat."

Chrissie just shook her head. There was no winning with her mom. "What's up with those photos you texted me in the middle of the night?"

"I didn't send you any photos."

"You did." Chrissie pulled out her phone to make her point. She displayed the photo of the sleeping bag for Flo.

"Crap." Flo pulled out her phone to check. She scowled. "Dammit. I meant to send this to my friend Chris. We should have given you a proper girl's name."

Chrissie just shrugged. Occasionally, she would be the inadvertent recipient of an email intended for someone named Chris. But it didn't happen often enough to bug her.

"Now I'm gonna lose my bet."

"What bet?" Chrissie wondered aloud. It seemed liked she had landed in Flo's wonderland. None of this made sense to her.

"I was supposed to text Chris evidence before four a.m. or else it doesn't count. Danggit!"

"Who's this Chris guy, anyway?"

"Someone I met while I was locked up."

"You mean... when you were in the hospital."

"Yes. Same thing."

"It couldn't have been that bad. I mean, they must have given you some pretty good sedatives."

"Spoken like someone who has built their own true cage of predictability. You sit in your apartment cage, only to drive your car cage to your cubicle cage. You wouldn't know the difference between the mundanity of your life and the mundanity of being locked up."

Chrissie thought her mom was being pretty harsh with her. Her lip pouted.

"Sorry," Flo said. "I'm not used to being in close proximity to normal people."

Chrissie looked away, avoiding eye contact. "It's okay. Me and my cages will... just remained caged."

"Look, why don't you stay for dinner tonight? I haven't eaten the chicken you bought me. We could heat it in the oven and maybe even watch a movie together. Pop some Jiffy Pop like old times?"

The offer pulled on Chrissie's heartstrings. She couldn't deny the nostalgia of hanging out together, pretending there was no rift between them. Besides, she had to eat. "Yeah, okay. Sounds good. Just don't let your cage bump my cage."

Flo laughed at the joke, which made Chrissie feel even more special. It was almost like they were old friends.

They went into the house and Chrissie started preparing the food, turning the oven to 350 degrees. Flo sat on the kitchen island, looking through her mail.

"Your lock is acting up. I couldn't get inside the house using my key."

Flo peered over her eyeglasses at her. "I changed the locks."

Chrissie nearly dropped the chicken. "What? How am I supposed to check on you if I can't use my key to get into the house?"

"It didn't stop you today."

Chrissie winced. Her mom had dodged the question.

Flo said, "You know that the back sliding door is always unlocked. But you know what? Most people don't, and I've had the same lock for decades. I just want to be safe. I'm alone here."

Chrissie put her hands on her hips and scolded Flo with her eyes.

Flo flailed her hands and got up from her seat, rummaged in the side drawer, and pulled out a key. She slapped it on the counter. "Here you go. But when all this nonsense about babysitting me is over, I want that copy back. You never know, I might want to have a boyfriend over one of these days."

Chrissie laughed. She took the key and added it to her key ring. "Babysitting you got us back together."

"You make us sound like we're a rock band or something."

"It's nice to be connected again. To be in the house. My room looks exactly as it did when I was growing up."

"Some things shouldn't change. They say the constant in life is change, but if some things can stay the same, I say why not?"

"It's nice that you kept my stuffed animals."

"I even kept that one doll that you cried so fitfully about losing. Remember?"

"Lola the Cabbage Patch doll. How could I forget? You basically told me to get over it."

"Well, it *is* just a doll. I lost Giovanni and *I* had to get over it. Maybe I wasn't the kindest about the whole ordeal. But you know, life's fucking tough, and everyone just expects you to get on with it." She went silent for a moment, then said, "It was hard. No one held me while I cried and told me it would all be okay. I had to tough it out."

Chrissie didn't buy that. "What, so since no one did that for you, you felt it was okay not to do that for me?"

"Chrissie." Flo caught her breath as she choked back tears. "I wanted you to be tough so you could handle anything. I didn't want you to break into a million pieces like I did when tragedy struck. I thought that if I gave you some tough love, you'd become independent and figure out life on your own terms. And honestly, it seems like you're doing fine."

Chrissie wanted to laugh with bitterness. She shrugged. "Sure. I'm okay. I'm a forty-year-old divorcée with a mediocre, hourly job. Yeah, other people are worse off, but I sure as hell haven't amounted to anything."

Out of nowhere, Flo took Chrissie's hands in her own. "You're doing good in my book. Look, as a mother I made some mistakes. I didn't always know what I was doing. Did you ever think you'd be better off without me? 'Cause I sure did." She started crying and walked away to grab a tissue.

Chrissie came around that side of the counter and caressed her mother's back. *Imagine comforting your mom for screwing up raising you. Talk about a catch-22.*

Flo wriggled at her touch, and Chrissie stopped consoling her. "Anyway, I'm trying to say *I* fucked up and *you're* doing good, kid." Flo wiped her eyes and shook her head. "That's enough of that. I hate crying. And Lord knows I've done enough crying for this lifetime."

"You lost your husband. You have a right to cry."

"It's not just that, you know. I loved your dad, but sometimes he got on my last nerve."

"Mom!"

"He did. You were married for a time, so you know how it is. You can be best buds one day and mortal enemies the next. It wasn't losing his companionship that hurt the most. What hurt so bad was the unfairness of it all. He was in his *thirties* when he died! Who gets dealt a hand like that, you know? And his daughter—you—were just a toddler. He left you without a father. Phew. It just killed me. That's when I severed my relationship with God. Why worship something that causes so much pain?"

Chrissie nodded. It made sense, even though she had never had a formal relationship—or severing of that relationship—with God. Hers was more an approach of indifference. She wasn't sure how she felt about God and wasn't one-hundred-percent sure God knew she was here. She might have just been an accidental spawn, no more important that a stick of bubblegum dropped out of someone's pocket.

"Then there's the depression," Flo said.

"You mean bipolar disorder, don't you?"

"It's the damn *depression*, Chrissie, that makes me feel heavy. These doctors don't know shit. All they say is 'chemical imbalance blah blah blah.' They don't know nothing else but that something's off with your brain. The so-called 'manic' part is me being fully myself. That's when I feel courageous, alive, unstoppable. That's how humans should feel—not stuffing themselves into..."

"Cages?" Chrissie ventured with a smirk.

"Yeah. Exactly. Have you seen how repressed some of these 'balanced' housewives are? Barely do anything if it's not in service to cooking, cleaning, caring for kids, or catering to a man's needs. It's a damn shame, it is. They don't even know they're suppressing their true desires. They don't have the *luxury* of 'manic phases,'" she said, gesturing with air quotes. "They're too busy being good little girls to know who they really are and what they really want."

Chrissie shrugged. She didn't know many housewives, but she guessed it was different living out here in the 'burbs. She did agree that she was so busy trying to fit in that she barely had an ounce of energy left over to stand out. And that was assuming she harbored anything within herself that desired to do so. Maybe she'd craved love and approval for so long that she'd forgotten about fulfilling any other desires.

"Look at me preaching," Flo said. "I should have a talk show or something. Is that chicken ready? I'm starving."

Chrissie pulled it out of the oven and grabbed the mashed potatoes from the microwave. "Looks good. No vegetables tonight, though."

"Ah, that's okay. I eat enough Jell-O as it is... That's a veggie, right? Hey, slap some butter on those potatoes, will you?"

"I think they already have some on there."

"Great. Add some more. You're only forty, what are you worried about—cholesterol? You're going to die some way or another... may as well enjoy yourself now."

Chrissie grabbed the butter out of the fridge and carved out a chunk. "I'm sure that attitude didn't help Dad's aneurysm."

"Fate is fate is fate," Flo intoned. "Maybe we could have stopped it, maybe we couldn't have? Who knows. Speaking of, maybe we should watch the movie *The Butterfly Effect*?"

"Sure. I haven't seen it."

"Heh. I'll get the TV trays." Flo went to the hallway closet and pulled out two old metal tray stands and put them in front of the couch. "Should we open that bottle of cabernet you brought?"

"Yeah. It's okay for you?"

"No biggie. I already took my lithium earlier today. Surprised you didn't check my pills, actually. Anyhow, I'm sure I won't die from a solitary glass of wine."

Chrissie brought each of them a solid pour of red wine in two stemmed wine glasses she found in the kitchen cupboards. Flo put on the movie and started devouring her food. Chrissie followed suit. She'd forgotten how much she enjoyed a good rotisserie chicken with its crunchy skin and tender meat. It reminded her of a home-cooked meal, which she hadn't made in a while. Everything she ate these days was either microwaved or prepackaged. She just didn't want to spend energy on much more than opening a bottle of wine when she got home from work.

She wasn't sure about the movie, although it was thought-provoking, and Ashton Kutcher was candy to the eyes. It told a story about him trying to change his present life by going back to the past, which resulted in constant undesirable changes in the new future. Even with the movie's warnings, Chrissie certainly wished she could go back and change her past. She'd attempt to get her dad to a doctor before he died. She'd take some classes about marriage and relationships before accepting an impromptu proposal and getting hitched. She'd have at least prayed for a miracle for her mom's depression and mood swings growing up instead of cowering in hopelessness. Maybe doing these things wouldn't have changed her life's trajectory, but imagining the possibilities gave her hope.

She looked over at Flo. Her wine glass was empty and her head was tilted back against the couch cushion. She was snoring softly. Chrissie covered her with a blanket and continued watching the movie at a lower volume. She didn't really have to stay, but it was nice having company, even if that person was in the dream realm. Her mom was nearby and they weren't bickering. This felt like progress.

When the movie ended, Chrissie placed the plates in the kitchen sink and put away the TV trays. She recalled the slew of laundry waiting to be attended to and returned to the laundry room where she folded clean towels and placed another load in the washer. There was something wholesome and real about being in her childhood home and helping her mom with basic things like dinner and laundry.

Before loading the whites into the washer, she first removed a blouse that had eyelet detail so she could handwash it. She hadn't bothered to handwash anything of hers in forever because she purposefully never bought or owned anything that required that much attention. Stretchy jeans and washable tops were her friends. Still, she hadn't forgotten how to wash things individually. That was a lesson she had learned growing up and hadn't forgotten.

She got the bottle of Woolite out of the cupboard, poured some into the sink, and filled it with cold water. She dunked the blouse into the liquid and gently washed it. Pulling it out of the water, she scanned it for any stains or areas that needed more attention, then washed it again and rinsed it with fresh water. She drained the shirt and hung it over the sink to dry.

The tile floor in the laundry room was tugging at Chrissie's OCD. Dust and fibers scattered here and there were begging to be swept. She grabbed the broom out of the linen closet in the hallway and began to sweep the laundry room. *Too bad I never get this motivated to clean my own apartment.*

She noticed clumps of dryer lint between the two machines and contorted her body to get at them. Wedging the broom sideways in the gap, she pulled inward several times and was rewarded with hunks of gunk. She got the dustpan out to collect the pile off the floor. When she went to empty it into the trash can, Chrissie noticed something flat in the mixture of debris and pulled it out carefully with her index finger and thumb.

She dumped the gunk in the trash, then went to the study where the lighting was bright so she could figure out what she'd discovered. The object was dusty, but she realized with a start that it was an old Polaroid picture. She ducked underneath the overhead light to inspect it. The photo had faded quite a bit and it was hard to make out the details.

She squinted and thought she saw the faint outline of bell-bottom jeans. There was mid-length hair... a pier... a girl. It was Chrissie and her dad at the Santa Monica pier when she was little! A stranger would hardly be able to determine what this photo captured, but Chrissie saw the faint outline of people and remembered the day exactly as she'd lived it.

She pulled the photo close and held it to her heart. Time seemed frozen. She sighed, and light tears filled her eyes. *What a relief. Something of my father still exists in this world.*

Time flowed once more, and her mind began to race. Why was this photo in the laundry room? Had Flo missed it, or purposely not destroyed every family photo with Giovanni in it?

Chrissie walked into the living room with the faded image in hand, intending to confront Flo about it. She found her mom still sound asleep on the couch. Chrissie stopped short of shaking her awake.

She looked down at the photo and decided to ask Flo about it another time. She was asleep and they'd just had *one evening* of peace between the two of them, rarer than a unicorn. It could wait. Chrissie tucked the Polaroid into her purse. She wasn't going to ask about it now, but she was certainly going to keep the photo. She deserved that much.

It was just past eight o'clock and Chrissie thought she should be heading home to get some sleep before the start of work. *Should I wake up Flo or just sneak out the front door?* Either option seemed kind of rude to her, and Chrissie didn't want to upset the delicate balance they'd achieved that night.

She sat down for a minute and thought about her decision. She realized there was a third option: She could sleep in her old room, then leave super early in the morning to get to work on time. Did she want to do that? It seemed extreme. She looked over at Flo, who was sleeping soundly.

This is my one and only mother. If she's not worth it, who is?

Chrissie had already made her decision, she just had to commit to it. What would this look like? She didn't have a change of clothes, but what she wore was comfortable enough to sleep in. She knew where the stash of toothbrush supplies was from her earlier exploration and she'd bet there was at least one unopened toothpaste tube in the bathroom cabinet. She would leave at the crack of dawn before her mom woke, go home to shower and change, then drive to work.

And that was that.

Chrissie moved her purse to her childhood bedroom, then placed a few decorative pillows and a teddy bear to one side of the bed so there was space for her to lie down. She propped her head on a fluffy pillow, pulled up a Kindle book on her phone, and started reading.

She started to nod off almost immediately, her head tilting to one side and sliding off the pillow. She was aware of her own snoring which woke her up periodically before dozing off completely.

Her dreams were vivid, like she had been dropped into a movie. She was having a dramatic conversation with her boss, The Griper, who in the dream world was represented as a little librarian wearing a pulled-back bun and horn-rimmed glasses. Chrissie was explaining to her the situation about her mom—which made no sense, since she didn't even like Vanessa, much less trust her. Chrissie went on and on about how her father had died young, when she was just a child, and her mother became unbalanced not long after, telling stories of times like when Flo forgot to take her to school and left her alone at home, asleep in her bedroom. She told The Griper of how Flo was diagnosed with bipolar disorder, and of the time her aunt Michelle told her in that weird way adults speak to children that her mother wasn't feeling well—though Michelle wasn't really her aunt by relation but instead an "adopted" family member Flo had met at the local Catholic church.

Michelle had told her Flo would be taking medicine for a long time to help her feel better, and that if Chrissie ever needed help with anything, she could call her auntie. At that moment Chrissie hadn't really understood what her aunt was saying, but she listened and nodded like a good girl. Later in her bedroom, she'd cried because she didn't think the medication was helping—her mom remained forgetful and distant.

Her dreams went on and on. She was transported to a picnic table. Her dad was sitting across from her. She imagined she was dreaming of heaven because she was her actual age while her dad looked just a bit older than he would have when he'd died in his thirties. They were sharing a spread of freshly made capicola and cheese. She couldn't understand their conversation but at the end he mouthed a clear, "I'm proud of you, Chrissie."

The dream shifted. She felt like Alice in Wonderland, searching among several large wooden doors for the right door to help her find Flo while frantically repeating out loud to herself, "I have to take care of my mother, I have to take care of my mother."

Chrissie woke up suddenly, disoriented by her surroundings. She sat up and wiped her eyes. She was in her childhood bedroom. No more dreamland. It was 5 a.m.

It seemed ridiculous to be up and moving at this early hour, but Chrissie knew that by 6 a.m. she absolutely had to get going or risk being late to work. And she was sick of Vanessa's abusive attitude toward her—she didn't want to give her any reason to justify her cruelty.

Chrissie stayed in bed. "Just a few more minutes," she whispered. Her eyes closed.

She woke up to the sound of crying. Startled, she scrambled out of bed. She walked down the hallway into the living room. She stood aloof as she watched her mom, sitting on the couch, sobbing silently into her hands. It felt like a private moment Chrissie wasn't supposed to see. She was unsure whether she should move and attempt to comfort her mom or head back to her bedroom for a bit to give her some privacy.

She remembered her words from her dream: *I have to take care of my mother.* Maybe this was a sign that she really needed to be there for Flo.

She tapped the wall lightly to let Flo know she was nearby. "I'm sorry to bother you," Chrissie said.

"Oh, Chrissie. I'm so down, so alone," Flo sputtered, crying into her hands again.

She sat down next to her mother and lightly rubbed her back.

Rocking back and forth, Flo said, "All I wanted to do was something exciting, something that made me feel alive. The doctors, they give me meds and say I should be 'balanced,' but then I just feel down." She wiped her tears with the back of her hand and seemed to grab hold of her composure. She hesitated, then continued, "I feel bold and alive when I'm... what they refer to as *manic*. If life is going to look gray and boring all the time, I don't know that I want to experience it."

Chrissie's heart ached for her mother, yet she understood some of what she said. Chrissie rarely felt roaringly alive in her day-to-day existence. It was moments like being at happy hour listening to good music, or going on a sexy date—or really, anything that involved drinking—that made her come alive. She didn't think she was manic-depressive herself, but that most human beings probably struggled to feel good, connected, and fulfilled most of the time. Life was hard. So if Flo didn't enjoy feeling "normal and balanced," how could Chrissie blame her? Where was the incentive to take her medication and get well if that meant feeling worse off?

Chrissie shook her head. This line of thinking could be dangerous. She wondered if she should call the doctor. There must be some best practices for how to handle episodes like this.

Florence stopped crying and didn't say anything else. She nestled herself against the couch and stared at the wall. It made Chrissie worry about her even more.

"I'll stay with you, Mom."

I'll find a way, she vowed. She remembered some language in the documents she'd signed from Sepulveda Health Center. She still had the papers in her car's glove compartment. She went outside to her car and got the documents. At the kitchen counter, she scanned them. She found the section she was looking for:

You may be entitled to receive up to 12 weeks of unpaid, job-protected leave per year covered by the Family and Medical Leave Act (FMLA). The law may also enable you to receive paid leave for up to two weeks depending on your employer. It also requires your employer to maintain your group health care benefits during leave. This includes caring for an immediate family member (i.e., spouse, child, or parent) with a serious health condition...

Yes! This was what she was looking for. Finally, this inane piece of paper she'd been required to sign had some purpose. She scanned the full document with her iPhone, then uploaded it in an email. She hesitated, then compiled the email to go directly to Christine Chan in human resources, and cc'd her manager for awareness. FMLA in California was no joke. Chrissie was sure she'd be able to take at least a week or two of paid leave to care for her mother. She'd figure out the rest as she went along.

It was barely 6 a.m. and all Chrissie had to do was wait for work to respond while watching her mom. Flo had fallen back asleep on the couch. That reprieve worked for Chrissie. *What a relief it is to skip work today and not have to battle with traffic on the 405 freeway.*

She went back to her bedroom and, leaving the door wide open, returned to a dreamless sleep.

Chrissie awoke a few hours later to the sound of clanking in the kitchen and her mom's singing voice belting out the lyrics to "Singin' in the Rain."

"I'm siiingin' in the rain, just siiingin' in the rain. What a glooorious feeling, I'm haaappy again..."

Chrissie wasn't a morning person, and the idea of speaking to anyone right now terrified her. Would she be up to the task of helping her mother? What should she even do? She'd have to call the doctor and learn more about how she could help. Otherwise, she'd just be taking a much-needed break from work. That was fine with her, but she did want to provide support for her mother.

She checked her email while lying in bed. Human resources had replied to her email with a very formal response that reeked of legalese. That was good. It meant they were taking her very seriously. Ms. Chan had attached a variety of documents and indicated that Chrissie could use her sick time followed by vacation time to take two weeks of paid time off. All she had to do was fill out the forms she'd provided and send them back to the company for processing.

She could probably print all those documents on her mom's printer and send them over. Chrissie replied to the email that she had received Ms. Chan's response and would get the signed paperwork over to them later today. *Ha! Take that, Vanessa!* Now that bitch could set up her own PowerPoint presentations and find someone else to abuse. At least for a few weeks, Chrissie was off the hook.

Chrissie realized something very clearly at that moment: She hated her job. She disliked the boring work she did, loathed her boss, and gnashed her teeth during every commute. Even though she was only about eight miles from the office, it took a grueling twenty minutes of aggravating bumper-to-bumper traffic on La Cienega to get there. And that was on a *good* day. By the time she'd get ready for work and figure out breakfast, she was already flustered and running a few minutes late. By the time she got to the office parking lot, she was already *so* over it.

What would be a better work situation for me? That was a great question. She didn't know. She imagined her first answer was what many people wished for at first glance: to win the lottery and be instantly, obscenely wealthy. Then what would she do with her time? Probably a lot of daytime drinking at a local bar, singing karaoke, and passing out early. That would be a fun change of pace, at least for a while.

Chrissie stuck her tongue between her lips, lost in a reverie. She really should take up journaling. It would probably help her clear her head and figure out what she wanted from life and work. For the time being, she was admittedly grateful she worked for a by-the-book employer who honored FMLA and would pay her to care for her mother, and also honor her health benefits. She didn't plan to go to the doctor any time soon, but you never knew when you'd need coverage.

She recalled that she'd emailed a therapist almost a week ago to see if her insurance covered treatment but didn't remember getting a response. She checked her inbox. Nothing there. But in her spam folder, an email was waiting. Cynthia Bhatti had replied. The universe was complicated. It directed Chrissie to seek out a therapist, then hid her response in a spam folder. *Ironic.*

Deep down, Chrissie knew she wanted someone to talk to and help her figure things out. But she wasn't overly eager to get started. The process felt so *hard.* She opened the email from Dr. Bhatti. The email stated that Chrissie's insurance did cover sessions—Chrissie would have to cover the co-pay, but that was an affordable twenty bucks. The doctor had one appointment available, but Chrissie had to confirm soon. The delay in receiving her email meant she would have an appointment *this* week.

Ugh. That's too much pressure.

Chrissie probably wouldn't be mentally prepared, but what the hell. She could always chicken out and cancel. She replied to Cynthia and requested the upcoming appointment.

What a life milestone! I should post about this on social media: "Forty-Year-Old Starts Therapy!" And load it with a bunch of silly emojis. Chrissie giggled. This was her life now. She was her mother's caregiver *and* seeking professional help.

At that moment, Flo entered her room with a mixing bowl in hand. "No need to stay with me, Chrissie. I'm feeling way better! I'm making cookies. They'll be ready soon. You can take some home with you!"

And just like that, Flo waltzed out of the room, leaving Chrissie feeling more confused than ever. Since she didn't have to go to work and was feeling groggy, she simply remained in bed, cozy amongst the covers.

Hiding from the world.

She rolled over and woke to the smell of chocolate chip cookies, one of the most enticing scents in the world. Her mom had left a plate of cookies in the room. The rich, warm scent of cooked dough and chocolate lit up her brain like fireworks. She sat up and devoured one cookie in two quick bites.

Gosh, homemade cookies are so good.

There was a part of her that was giddy about waking up in her childhood bed filled with old blankies and stuffed animals, a plate of her mom's cookies by her bedside. She figured it was the same for every forty-year-old that didn't feel grown up and wished they could occasionally avoid adulting, if only for a few hours. The same part of her that felt unequipped to muddle through adulthood and wondered how she'd even made it this far.

She liked the idea of taking it a bit easier than usual, and wondered if she was using her mother's illness as an excuse for much-needed downtime. Chrissie pushed the thought away quickly. What difference did it make, anyway? California law and her company alike allowed her this time off. Whatever the outcome, she should savor easy, pleasant moments like this.

She sat up and stretched her arms and her neck, stiff from sleeping in so long. *It was still worth it*, she thought as she walked into the kitchen, trying to figure out her next move. She didn't have a change of clothes on her and was starting to feel greasy.

"Hey, Mom. What are you up to?"

"I got inspired and picked up a few things from the grocery store when you were asleep. Now I'm making banana muffins. They had a good-sized pile of ripened bananas, so I'm making two pans full. One with chocolate chips, and one without." She smacked her lips.

Chrissie smiled. "Sounds tasty. I was able to take two weeks off work to stay with you. I just need to go home and shower, get some clothes to change into."

Flo waved her off. "Nah. You can shower here. There are some clothes of mine in your closet that might fit you. I bought a few things at my favorite thrift store then decided they weren't my style, but couldn't bring myself to get rid of them."

Chrissie shrugged. A shower and a cuppa joe would do her good. She'd be able to think more clearly. "Okay. I'll check them out and shower. Then I have to go to Starbucks for a cup of coffee."

"Sounds splendid. I'll join you."

The closet held half a dozen items on hangers. There was a cute pair of faded blue bootcut jeans that she liked, and a V-neck, tie-dyed tank that was soft and billowy. They would work fine so long as they fit her.

She went to the hall closet to grab a towel—her mom had stored the towels in the same place in their house since the beginning of time. Then she proceeded to the guest bathroom and heated the water. While waiting, she found an extra deodorant and body lotion on the shelf under the sink. *We're in business.*

Chrissie hummed "Girls Just Wanna Have Fun" to herself while scalding-hot water trickled down her back.

She toweled off and put on the jeans—they fit remarkably well, the sides hugging her curvy hips while the stretchy material in front took pressure off her waist. When she looked at herself in the mirror, she felt more lighthearted than she had in a while.

Maybe I should have used my vacation time sooner on an actual vacation. Still, this isn't half bad.

She'd kept putting it off, saying she didn't have enough money or time or anyone to go with. Now here she was, taking an exotic vacation at her childhood home in the San Fernando Valley. This would be a ripe occasion for adding post-worthy pics to her Instagram profile. She rolled her eyes and chortled.

Chrissie entered the kitchen in her vintage jeans and top.

"You look cute!" Flo beamed.

"Thanks, Mom. It all fits really well."

"Good, good. I was thinking, maybe we could go for a full lunch at Weiler's Deli instead of just grabbing a coffee at Starbucks, since it's almost noon."

"Yum. I'm in."

Weiler's Deli was a local diner with Jewish staples: traditional matzoh ball soup and rugelach. More than anything, Chrissie loved their mile-high corned beef sandwiches on traditional rye bread that her mom had occasionally packed inside her school lunches all those decades ago. Whenever she got that sandwich for lunch as a child, stuffed in a brown paper bag direct from the deli, she knew there was something special inside.

They arrived at the Weiler's Deli parking lot and Chrissie parked her car close to the entrance. *No need for exercising on vacation, either.* When they entered, a waitress yelled out "Hi, Flo! Welcome!"

Her mom smiled big as a burly man with a thick mop of dark-brown hair and a beard waved them over to his booth. "Hey, Moof. This is my daughter, Chrissie."

"My pleasure, my pleasure, a-ha!" Moof extended a meaty hand to shake Chrissie's. He was a rather large fellow, and getting completely out of his booth to greet them required a fair amount of exertion.

Moof settled back down with a crash. Flo sat down opposite Moof once the booth stopped rocking and motioned Chrissie to join her. Chrissie wasn't sure she wanted to talk to a stranger, but she sat down anyway.

"I haven't seen you in a few weeks, Flo. How's everything going?"

"Oh, the dang mental police got me, saying I was in a manic-depressive state and needed treatment. I was in the hospital for almost two weeks!"

Chrissie found it curious to see how openly her mom spoke to this stranger about her problems. "Catholic Flo" from decades ago would have been afraid to mention anything about her mental illness for fear that neighbors would think less of her.

"A-ha, ain't that the worst! Well, we missed you. Glad you're back."

Chrissie didn't understand his use of the word *we*, unless he meant everyone in the restaurant.

The waitress came over and Flo ordered them both a cup of coffee. That's when Chrissie realized her mom was settling in—they would be dining with Moof. She instantly felt resentful; wasn't she was enough for her mom? Couldn't they sit in a booth by themselves together?

Flo gestured at Chrissie. "Do you want to look at the menu, honey?"

She hadn't been called *honey* in ages. The last time was probably when she'd traveled to New Orleans and gallivanted through the streets with a Hurricane in tow.

"I already know what I want. My favorite: the corned beef Reuben."

"Good choice," Moof said.

Chrissie didn't acknowledge his comment. What was he trying to be, her best friend or something?

They placed their food order and Chrissie sipped her cup of coffee and watched Flo and Moof chat. They seemed like old, good friends.

Her curiosity got the best of her. "How did you two meet?" Chrissie inquired.

Moof smirked and looked at Flo. "Permission to tell?"

Flo nodded that he could spill the beans. He swelled with excitement like a big, overblown school kid. *This should be good*, Chrissie thought.

"So here I was, sitting outside the Starbucks in Granada Hills, people-watching and reading stuff on my phone when this *radiant* brunette walks past wearing a stunning deep-red sweater. Out of nowhere, the lady sits down and huffs about the price of coffee, then sips her fancy latte with extra foam with her legs crossed and her pinky up. Eventually, I couldn't contain myself. I just had to say hello and ask her if she would ever allow a big lug like me to buy her a fancy cup of joe so that she didn't have to endure the suffering of paying for it. A-ha!"

He chuckled deeply. Flo was smiling. Chrissie didn't understand why, but they seemed to appreciate each other.

"To my surprise she said *yes*, and asked me if I wanted to join her. Of course, I *am* a smart enough man to know when to acquiesce. So, I moved my chair over to her table and we just talked and talked for hours. I had to go back inside to get us sandwiches because we grew so famished. We ended up talking until it got dark outside, at which point we finally exchanged phone numbers and said our goodbyes."

Chrissie was thoroughly confused. "Are you two, um... *dating*?"

The food arrived at that moment, which delayed the answer. Moof didn't respond quickly with a *no*, which Chrissie took to be a dark omen.

Flo said, "Sometimes two people just have a great connection and you've got to go with it."

When did my mom become an open-minded guru?

Chrissie doused her fries with Tabasco sauce and dipped one in ketchup. She focused extra hard on the food, feeling suddenly weird and not wanting to make eye contact for the moment.

Moof smiled and said, "I'm married but was meant to be in the priesthood. I missed my calling. Your mom told me about her husband from long ago, and about being diagnosed with bipolar, and having a daughter. She didn't talk to you much at that time. I guess that's finally changed?"

Moof peered at Chrissie as though offering his stamp of moral approval for her behavior towards Flo. She didn't like that. There were still parts of her that resented her mom. She wondered if this pseudo-priest could see through her with his prying eyes.

She gobbled up a big bite of her Reuben sandwich and filled her mouth with enough rye, sauerkraut, and meat that she couldn't respond to him. She just chewed and chewed, the silence at the table stretching out.

The others took it in stride. Flo dug into her stack of pancakes and stuffed a piece of bacon into her mouth. Moof took his toasted everything bagel and piled on lots of cream cheese and fresh tomato slices. He picked occasionally at an ample side of bacon, just for kicks.

He held out a greasy hand. "Anyone want a piece of crispy bacon?"

Despite her attempts to reject him, bacon was one of her weak spots and Chrissie took up his offer without hesitation. She grabbed the biggest piece she could find and started nibbling on it like a squirrel chowing down its prize nut. In between bites she offered a trite smile, just to be good mannered about the whole thing.

"Losing Giovanni when I was a young mother was difficult," Flo said. "Being lonely as a middle-aged woman was even harder. When I was younger, I was afraid of people—what they would think of me, if they'd be critical of me, whether they could be trusted. As I aged, I realized nothing is worse than being lonely all the time because you won't open up to people and give them a try."

The more she heard her talk, the more Chrissie thought she didn't know her mother at all. How could she? Most of their adult interactions had been clashes or disagreements of some sort. She'd never stopped to ask her mother how things were going beyond her illness, or what she enjoyed in her life. Then again, she didn't recall Flo asking her about these things either. *I guess you have to stay in touch to have those conversations.* All Chrissie had left of her family was her mother, and they had been disconnected for so long. *Why? I should have cherished Flo more instead of focusing on all her negative traits.*

As if he could see Chrissie's internal struggle, Moof interjected, "Sometimes it's hardest with the ones close to us. Connections sometimes feel easier with strangers than family."

Chrissie shrugged. She wasn't feeling connected to much of anything or anyone these days. Was there a time she'd really felt connected to others? When she thought back, she always felt she'd had a great relationship with her dad. But that was so long ago. Maybe she had glossed over it and their relationship had become cloaked in nostalgia. Nowadays, she was simply pretending to play the role of functional human being and getting through each day.

She sank her teeth into her sandwich. She didn't want to talk about this anymore—she didn't want to open up with some random stranger who thought he was Dr. Phil.

Moof and Flo talked about new buildings constructed at the Cal State University Northridge campus down the street. The Soraya Performing Art Center had enriched the area and anchored the campus as an architectural gem right on Nordhoff Street. It conveyed the impact of the public university on the San Fernando Valley, made possible by a generous donation from the Armenian couple Younes and Soraya Nazarian. The arts center and other permanent, more sophisticated buildings replaced temporary bungalows that had been erected after the 1994 Northridge earthquake had toppled many on-campus structures.

Chrissie started to zone out as they talked away, feeling like she was disappearing further into the abyss of her own mind.

A voice snapped her back to the present. "Chrissie, can we exchange numbers? That'll help us keep an eye on your mom." Moof winked as he grabbed the check from the table.

Chrissie had tired of his kitschy, desperate approach to making friends, but saved his number in her phone just in case. Flo's neighbor, Anne, had come across as somewhat indifferent. That was one thing Moof was not. He seemed to care a little *too* much about her mom. Despite his annoying personality, Chrissie figured he was harmless. And he could be helpful if Chrissie ever needed insight into her mom's behavior or whereabouts.

They said their goodbyes to the big lug and drove back home. Chrissie kept the car running as her mom exited the vehicle.

Flo looked back at her questioningly. "Are you coming?"

Chrissie shook her head. "I should go home and get some things of my own."

"Don't be silly. It's late afternoon and there will already be traffic. Go get some clothes tomorrow. I have the cutest lounge set you can try on. Never been worn. You can get cozy and watch a movie or read a book. Enjoy your vacation time."

Eating that big sandwich had left Chrissie feeling drowsy, and she certainly wasn't ready to deal with the 405. She put the car in park and turned off the ignition. Her mind was wrung out. She felt like a zombie, walking through her day without meaningful conscious thoughts. Maybe her mom was right about her needing the down time.

The lounge set was indeed comfy—a soft cotton material with a soothing sky-blue-and-pink watercolor pattern. Once Chrissie put it on, she decided she never wanted to wear jeans again. She idly wondered if her mother had secretly been stashing things in her size just in case they would one day reconcile. The amount of stuff she had on hand that happened to fit Chrissie perfectly was becoming suspect. But as she sipped on a White Claw she'd picked up at the liquor store on their way home, she cared less and less about the meaning behind it all and became more and more interested in putting her feet up on the ottoman.

"I need you to remind me to take my pills every night at eight p.m. this week," Flo belted from the kitchen. "I have lithium and a magnesium supplement I'm allowed to take to help me sleep."

"'K, will do." Chrissie set a daily recurring reminder on her phone to make sure she wouldn't forget.

Flo said, "What did you think of Moof?"

"He's alright. Seems to like you quite a bit."

"He's very attentive and a good listener. He's a kind man, Chrissie."

"Well, if you like him then I trust that sentiment."

Silence was better than an argument over feelings Chrissie didn't totally understand. She was still downloading all the impressions she'd been absorbing while sitting at lunch with the two of them.

"I'm going to take a nap," Flo said. "Are you comfy?"

Chrissie smiled. "These PJs are to die for."

"Then you should keep them. They look great on you. I just might have bought them at Marshalls with you in mind a while ago." Flo looked at Chrissie, her eyes watering. "I know we've had our challenges, Chrissie, but I'm glad we're getting some time together now. I'm going to keep taking my meds. I'll be fine. I mean, I've always been just fine. But it's nice to have you here, and I'm glad you're taking a break from work."

Chrissie didn't want to start crying right now. She didn't want to feel her feelings. She managed a smile and mouthed a *thank you* that channeled her feelings and allowed her to suppress her tears. Flo went into her bedroom and shut the door.

The ceiling fan whirred in the background, creating a murmur of white noise that—together with her drink—put her into a relaxed state of being.

Chapter 4: Dive

Chrissie woke up an hour later with a dry mouth and groggy eyes. Her phone was pinging a message notification. It was Becky from work: *What's going on with you? I saw you're not at your desk. You haven't been fired, have you? I didn't want to say anything because people think I know what's up with you. Please text me!*

At first, Chrissie wasn't sure how to reply. Obviously, she still had a job... she just wasn't eager to return to it. After thinking for a moment, she finally crafted a reply: *Thanks for checking on me. I took FMLA at home with my mother because she wasn't feeling well. Should be back in two weeks.* She sent the message and then followed it up with another: *Staying in the SFV, if you want to explore local dive bars.* The bait was set. If they went to a bar, her mother would likely be asleep the whole time anyway, so she wouldn't be shirking her responsibility.

That thought reminded Chrissie that she should call Flo's doctor. The contract she'd signed listed Dr. Reynolds as Flo's primary caregiver at Sepulveda Health Center. She punched his number into her phone and called. The person who answered didn't understand what she was saying and put her on hold. She listened to several minutes of boring music before someone picked up.

"This is Jess."

"Hello, I was trying to get ahold of Dr. Reynolds. He was my mom's doctor while she was in the facility."

"I'm sorry, we don't have a Dr. Reynolds here."

What? That can't be right.

"He was watching over my mom, Florence Demata. She stayed there last week."

"I'm sorry, but if you want patient records or to speak with someone about patient care, you'll have to submit a form online with your request and proof of your relationship to the patient."

Jess paused for a second. Chrissie fumed in silent frustration. "Hello?" Jess said.

"I'm here. You guys sure don't make this easy."

"Sorry. It's HIPAA regs."

There was another pause. *Screw this*, thought Chrissie. "'K. Thanks," Chrissie said tersely and hung up. She was furious and confused. How could they not have the doctor there that had just issued a contract she'd signed? If the doctor wasn't there any longer, they usually told you that. Maybe he was originally at Northridge Hospital where her mom had been first committed? *How inefficient!*

She searched on her phone, *How to help someone with bipolar*. The results weren't very helpful.

"The ups and downs can be difficult." *No duh!*

"Encourage them to seek help and to take their medication regularly. Bipolar is typically a lifelong disorder that requires patience and treatment to develop stabilization strategies for mood swings. Try to reduce stress in the patient's environment and know everyone involved has limitations. Getting well is in the hands of the person with the illness, so be patient and supportive."

Chrissie read a little longer before tossing her phone on the coffee table. She was feeling hopeless. All the guidance she could find online told her to be patient, roll with the punches, and ensure the person was following their treatment regimen. Maybe just being here with her mother was enough? Apparently that was all she could do—it *had* to be enough.

She kept wishing she was at happy hour. That seemed to be one thing Chrissie could control in her own life. There was happy hour *somewhere* nearby, and she had the power to get herself to it. Heck, it was almost five o'clock—the golden hour. She thought for a moment about her clothes situation, then remembered she could use her new bootcut jeans to be cute and probably find some sort of earrings lying around the house to spruce up her outfit. She didn't need to get dolled up like Dolly Parton, she just needed to feel cute enough to go out in public. And by "go out in public," she meant a dark, skeevy San Fernando Valley dive bar where the lighting worked in a forty-year-old's favor. There were times for good lighting. This wasn't one of those times.

She had decided to head out, even if that meant going by herself tonight. She didn't expect Becky to join her way out here on a weeknight.

It was then that she realized Flo was in the room with her—she had snuck in like a ghost.

Flo smiled. "You look deep in thought. What's up?"

Chrissie grimaced. "Um, I thought you were going to take a nap? I was thinking about the most important time of the day: happy hour." She gave a chuckle that quickly died off. *One day I'll have more to aspire to.*

"Sounds fun. Where are you going? Who's meeting you there?"

"Sherman Oaks… somewhere. And no one's meeting me. It'll just be me and my long-term relationship with wine and music."

"Hmm. Interesting." Flo looked down and started messing with her phone.

"Mom. What are you doing?"

"Welp, good news: Moof has agreed to drive us around town, so no DUIs for us tonight!"

Chrissie leaned forward, wringing her hands. "You'll join me? Won't that be weird?"

"Hey, I'm human and I like to be around other people. Why would that be weird?"

"I don't know. Mom and daughter, drinking it up together like two single college gals?"

"That's one way things could go. What exactly were you thinking of getting up to tonight? Planning on making the morning paper with your scandals?"

"Ha. Perhaps. I guess it'll just be us old bags swinging our crochety hips from side to side while drinking a Tom Collins."

"I don't know what a Tom Collins is."

"It's what all the old ladies are drinking these days." Chrissie winked.

"You're a bit sarcastic for a woman your age. Wait until you hit your sixties before you break out the big guns." Flo's phone pinged. "It's done. He'll pick us up at four forty-five so we can get to happy hour right when it starts."

"Cool." Chrissie paused, then said, "You really like him? Moof?"

"Eh, it's nice to have someone drive you around town and listen to you talk. It's a better relationship than many of my friends' marriages."

"Alright. I like the idea of being chauffeured and not having to pay for it, so I guess that's a win. I just didn't know you had friends."

"Shush, you. Seems your new name tonight is 'Snarky' instead of 'Chrissie.' And I *do* have friends, but many don't live close, and you know how you just drift apart." Flo grew quiet.

"What is it, Mom?"

Flo shook her head. "No, it's nothing. Just thinking of an old friend. I know I make being bipolar look easy and fun, but it can be hard." She sat down and sighed.

Forget Google, this is the perfect time to ask her directly... "How can I help you?"

Flo looked up and met her gaze. "Just being here means a lot. Even the doctor's prescribed meds can't prevent all my mood swings. It's just, I'm getting older and I'm not going to be around forever. I don't want to be the awful mother who died alone, with no one by her bedside to wish her well on the other side."

"Wow, okay. Your name tonight is 'Morbid.'"

Flo laughed.

"Seriously, though," Chrissie pressed, "you're not that old. Why are you feeling that way now?"

"Because of the lump in my breast that they tested. It's not cancer, by the way. What a relief! But it really made me think about my life. And that was around the same time as Giovanni's birthday, and I got so sad and sentimental. I know they say, 'time heals all wounds,' but it still feels fresh after all these years."

"Yeah. I've never gotten over him either. Shit happens." Chrissie waved her hand about like she was holding an imaginary wand. "Thus, happy hour."

"Guess it'll have to do."

Chrissie never imagined her life would be so glamorous that she'd have a rotund middle-aged man in a dark-purple minivan taking her and her mom out for drinks on a weeknight. Life really did have a sense of humor. Still, she acknowledged this was better than driving drunk or being out by herself. This was her new life.

They arrived at the Sugar Mill Saloon's parking lot—a gem nestled in a strip mall between retail shops and flanked by a Round Table Pizza. Then, in a rare show of chivalry for their era, Moof made them wait to exit until after he'd parked the van and could come around to help them out of the vehicle. Even for someone as excitable as him, he seemed particularly enthusiastic about the night's events.

He probably doesn't get out much, Chrissie thought.

She led the way, arm in arm with her mom. She almost felt like they were becoming friends of sorts. Luckily the bar had plenty of open seats and they took up three barstools in the corner next to a tabletop arcade. Apparently Moof liked to play card games on the tablet while hanging out. *To each their own.* Chrissie found herself feeling uncharacteristically empathetic in the moment.

The bartender swung by, and Chrissie said, "Whiskey sour with Crown Royal, please."

"Starting off with the good stuff, huh? I was thinking simpler, like a glass of pinot grigio." Flo batted her eyes at the bartender, who started making their drinks.

Chrissie said, "I'm on vacation. There's nothing two ibuprofens can't fix."

"Here, here!" said Moof in jovial agreement. "A-ha!" He passed a few bucks over to her.

"What's this for?"

"I thought maybe you'd want to play some tunes on the jukebox."

Chrissie nodded in approval. Music was good. *Why not?* She took a sip of her whiskey sour, covered it with a napkin—a habit developed from drinking alone at bars—and went to the jukebox to select some songs.

Classic rock was always a winner in her book. They were the type of songs that made you throw your hands up in the air and swing your hips when the booze took over your bloodstream. She started with "LA Woman" by The Doors, Elton John's bar favorite "Benny and the Jets," then a mix of Queen, Led Zeppelin, and a few classic Madonna songs to top off the fun.

She skipped lightheartedly on her way back to the bar.

"Someone's having fun, huh?" Flo sipped her white wine.

"*Jukeboxes* are fun." She smiled at Moof but couldn't bring herself to say thank you.

Moof called the bartender over. "Can I get an Old Grand-Dad?"

"Sure thing. Neat or rocks?"

"Neat, please." Moof smiled his goofy smile.

"What's an Old Grand-Dad?" Chrissie asked. "Seems fitting for you."

Her snark rolled off Moof like water. "It's a whiskey. *And* you're right, it's one of my nicknames."

"Ha. Moof's pretty easy to remember. Fewer syllables. I'll stick with that."

"Works for me, kiddo. A-ha!" He downed the drink and offered another cheesy grin.

"Is that it, old man? Just the one?"

"I can't drink too much with my diabetes, but one shot warms me up nicely. Then I switch to Diet Coke."

Chrissie didn't want to admit it, but she was warming up to his silly antics. There was no pressure, no expectation to behave a certain way around him. She was starting to understand a little more why Flo appreciated Moof's company. And it was becoming obvious there was nothing romantic between them, at least not from Flo's side. Moof seemed to be hopeful, yet probably understood on some level—with his thick, round glasses, mop of dark hair, and rotund body—he wasn't exactly oozing sex appeal. She guessed he was comfortable staying in the friend zone as it gave him proximity to attractive and vibrant women. He seemed to thrive off their energy. Like he enjoyed being a fly on the wall. He sat in the corner, watching, smiling, chatting, and playing some card game on the arcade machine.

Chrissie sucked up the watered-down ice at the bottom of her whiskey sour and ordered another. The first sips of a newly crafted sour were so tangy—she *loved* it.

"Benny and the Jets" came on and Chrissie started to sway her hips while seated.

"Let's go on the dance floor," Flo offered, taking Chrissie's hand.

Chrissie felt so in the flow, she almost didn't think about how uncool it was to be shaking her thing on a bar dance floor to '70s music on a weeknight. She suppressed her self-conscious desire to look cool and embraced enjoying herself. On the dance floor, the women moved their hips and waved their hands and laughed.

Their enthusiasm infected the entire room.

People joined them and formed a dance circle. Each person entered for a few seconds to show off their moves. No one judged, no one cared. Everyone wanted the chance to express themselves in a free environment, sloughing off the rules of the cubicles and anything else preventing them from being fully themselves.

Chrissie jumped into the center and did a booty shake followed by the running man and left the circle feeling hilariously in touch with humanity and her own joy. Maybe they were doing it all wrong? Maybe there was *too much* fitting into workspaces and rules and requirements and just not enough time to *be, express, experience.* Chrissie knew she was tired of sitting in a cookie-cutter cubicle, staring at spreadsheets and being mistreated by bosses. This moment was infinitely better.

Sweaty and exhilarated, Flo and Chrissie returned to their barstools, laughing together.

"That's the best therapy I've had in a long time," Flo said.

"That's the *only* therapy I've had in a long time," Chrissie chimed in.

"That looked like a lot of fun," Moof said. "I'd have joined you, but I would have been an elephant on the dance floor."

"No one would have minded, Moof," Chrissie replied, surprising herself by genuinely exuding kindness his way. Dancing hadn't just opened up her pores through sweat—it seemed to have affected her in ways she hadn't expected.

Her drink went down smooth. They always did. More rounds followed. The conversation was flowing. They were buying the bartender shots and visiting the dance floor repeatedly with their free-spirited, newly-made friends. All was right with the world.

Chrissie barely recalled the last few drinks. A foggy trip back to the house. A hazy walk down the hallway, and a comfy collapse onto her childhood bed. Yes, all was right with the world, and a good time was had by all. Especially Chrissie.

Chrissie heard a dull rumbling and woke to a bright beam of light lancing across in her face. She was disoriented and didn't know what time it was. Checking her phone, it was seven in the morning. Her mouth was pasty, and her head pulsed with tension. Disturbingly, she felt a yanking on her side.

"I have to get these covers washed. I have to wash the covers. You need to get up so I can clean them." Flo held Chrissie's bed sheets in both hands and was using all her body weight to pull them off the bed, with Chrissie still lying in it.

Chrissie blinked. Her hungover brain couldn't process what was happening. She sat up like a robot and said, "Let me help you."

"I don't need your help. I need you to *leave* so I can wash the sheets. I can do it myself! I'm an adult."

Chrissie suddenly found her emotions. "Okay," she bellowed. "Give me a second to get out of the bed then, for Christ's sake!"

She moved her feet to the edge of the bed and rubbed her temples. *Man, my head hurts.* Lacking a filter so early in the morning, she said, "If you're such an *adult* then why did the doctor ask me to be with you?"

"What *doctor* are you talking about?" Flo snarled. "You don't have to be here, you know. You could live your own life, take care of your own needs."

"*The* doctor! On the damn papers they made me sign when they dropped you off. You know, after your stay at the mental center?"

Flo grinned, and Chrissie felt her stomach sour. *What on earth is going on?* "Dr. Reynolds," she continued. "It's right on the contract I initialed and sent to my employer to take time off to care for you."

"You think you're so *smart*. There is no *Dr. Reynolds*. I made him up so you would stay with me. Chrissie, you *want* to be here with me, but you wouldn't take the first steps unless you felt like your hand was forced."

Chrissie couldn't believe what her mom was saying. "B-but the van driver... he handed me the papers. Everything is in lawyer-speak, it's totally official and my company accepted for FMLA. I don't understand what you're saying."

Flo stayed crouched at the edge of the bed, tightly gripping the sheets. "*We* created it. I told him I didn't want to die being estranged from my daughter. We took some blank papers from the main office at the center and googled some more stuff and made a realistic-looking contract. And look what happened!

You *wanted* it, Chrissie. You wanted to be here with your mother. You just needed a little push."

"I'm so confused. You lied to me? You had me take time off of work for... a big farce? A forgery?"

"You hate your job. Besides, you said they were paying you. So I helped you take a vacation." Flo stood there, hands on hips in manic defiance.

Am I trapped in some alcohol-fueled nightmare? This can't be true. "This is so wrong. Why didn't you talk to me honestly and just explain how you were feeling?"

"You don't *listen* to me. You're so frustrated and angry at me all the time. It's nearly impossible to have a moment to connect heart-to-heart with you."

"It's hard... you would never open your heart to me," Chrissie rebuked.

"Well, Chrissie, then we'll just agree to disagree. Now get out of *my* bed. It's time for you to leave so I can clean house."

"Seriously! Just like that?"

Chrissie felt a rage bubble up in her that made her hands shake. She did not have the damn patience for this bullshit. She stood up and looked squarely at the thin, spindly woman in front of her and felt absolute hatred.

"My whole life you begged me to support you, and you always left me hanging! You were never there for me. Now you want me to forgo my forties for you? I already gave you my childhood and lost most of my adult years to your insanity. Now you're telling me you tricked me into sacrificing everything because you needed me? Because you don't want to die alone?

"Well, *fuuuucccckkkk yooouuu*! I am so *tired* of giving up myself on your behalf, to the point that I don't even know who I am. I am done siphoning off my life force so you can feel whole. I *deserve* to become something! Whether it's good or bad or just existing, it doesn't matter—I deserve to stand wholly as myself, whoever the fuck that is. *I* get to decide if I want to accommodate your needs. *I* get to decide when I have enough left over to share and support you... or not! I won't be your energetic whipping girl! I deserve to have my own life, free from parasitism. I can't accept this dynamic. I can no longer sacrifice myself at the altar of your narcissism. This is it! I am done. Goodbye!"

Hands still shaking, Chrissie grabbed her phone and purse and stomped out of the house. She got in her car and screamed at the top of her lungs in rage. She pounded the steering wheel so hard the horn blared twice. "Fuck you! Fuck you! Fuck you! Damn you!" She sobbed into her hands. Her head pounded and her soul ached. How could her mother be so cold and thoughtless? How did she always manage to place her needs before Chrissie's? And how on earth did Chrissie always manage to fall for it?

What an idiot she was! She hated herself for believing her mother could love her. The idea that her mother could fully look at her and hear her needs was a big fat myth. A lie Chrissie had told herself for far too long. She had no idea what was coming next, but she was absolutely, completely, undeniably ready to live her life differently.

She had no idea how to change, but she knew now it wouldn't happen in the relationship with her mother. She wasn't hopeless—she was being brutally honest with herself.

The loving mother she'd always prayed and hoped for would never exist. Not now. Not with Flo. This really was the final goodbye.

Chrissie drove under the speed limit back to the Westside, her eyes watery, her head and heart spinning with emotion. What had just happened? She'd been pissed at being woken up so rudely, especially after a night of drinking. The more she thought about it, the situation made no sense. The night before with Flo had been filled with spontaneity and joy. What had happened to bring everything crashing down so abruptly?

Chrissie pulled into her carport and took a deep breath. She still felt sad, but her tears had run dry. She looked at her phone. No messages from Flo. No messages from anyone, really. Just empty silence. She checked her email. One message stood out: *Confirming our appointment today.*

Huh?! thought Chrissie. She read through the email in a panic. It was Dr. Bhatti confirming their appointment for this afternoon! Chrissie thought she'd scheduled for the end of the week. She did not want to talk *at all* today. She turned off her phone, stuffed it inside her purse, and traipsed up to her apartment where she could collapse into a sad, confused heap in the safety and privacy of her home.

Despite feeling distraught, she managed to ooze her way off the couch and into the shower. A shower could fix a lot of things. A bit of lotion here, a few essential oils there—in this case, a fragrant one infused with "rose oil for self-love" from a reiki healer on Etsy. And deodorant—what a miracle that was! For the first time in days, she felt squeaky clean, and better off for it.

She sat back down on the couch, noticing the heaviness still bearing down on her chest. Much had been released today, but it had left her with more confusion and uncertainty than relief.

She turned to her phone for a distraction. On Instagram, everyone was so freaking happy in all their posts with hair perfectly manicured, relationships all doing well, children sparkling with joy. One gal had posted a carefully curated image of her daily tarot card. Chrissie didn't know how people did it—post images so regularly that looked so consistently lovely and perfect. It was all too much for her. Tossing her phone, she realized she felt completely ungrounded and hadn't pulled a tarot card for herself in almost a week.

Chrissie was too exhausted to even ask the cards a question right now, much less contemplate its meaning. Instead, she fluffed up a pillow and leaned back on the couch, easily falling to sleep.

Her phone ringer loudly burst through her dreams. She sat up startled and feeling on edge, like she was about to repeat the morning's scuffle with her mother. *It's awful yet funny how traumatic experiences can be recalled so easily—the way my body braces for discomfort like it's reliving the experience all over again.*

She answered the phone, and unexpectedly found herself on FaceTime. Her reflection in the corner of her screen mortified her. Her face was red, she had a crease on one cheek, and her hair was down and unkempt.

"Hi, Chrissie. I'm Dr. Cynthia Bhatti."

Chrissie waved awkwardly. *Wow, I missed my actual appointment, but the doctor called me directly.* She had been hoping she could gloss over her flakiness and move on with her life sans therapist, but Dr. Bhatti wasn't having it.

Dr. Bhatti said, "We scheduled an appointment for you today. As I'm sure you know, it's your responsibility to show up to professional appointments that you book. We can take our hour together now over the phone instead."

Chrissie's brows rose. She was in shock. This lady was really putting her on the spot. "Okay?"

"Okay." Dr. Bhatti shuffled some papers on her desk, then peered right into the camera at Chrissie. "Tell me why you sought me out for therapy."

"Um. I can't fully remember why," Chrissie said, playing coy. "It's been a few weeks since I reached out."

"That's okay. Tell me what's going on in your life right now. I'll listen."

Do I have to do this? Chrissie took a deep breath and said, "Not much. I have a job I hate, and a mother who's... well..." She trailed off as her voice began to crack.

"Take your time, Chrissie."

Chrissie steeled herself. "My mother is bipolar. And she's manipulative. We had a huge fight this morning, and honestly, I'm just beside myself."

"That's why you didn't make it to today's appointment?" Cynthia said with sympathy.

Chrissie remained silent, allowing the question to hang in the air answered. She truly wished she could avoid ever opening up to anyone.

Dr. Bhatti continued, "Tell me more about your relationship with your mother."

"After my father died—a long time ago—my mom grew distant. Forgetful and neglectful. It was difficult for me because I didn't feel like I could lean on her for support or guidance. I mean, I was just a child." Speaking that last sentence aloud, her voice cracked again.

Cynthia nodded.

"We haven't talked much since I became an adult," Chrissie said. "A few weeks ago, she ended up in the hospital after a manic breakdown. The hospital called me. I was very reluctant to help, but also would have felt guilty if I didn't. They said I was the only one listed on her medical records. We don't have much family left around here."

Chrissie paused to take a breath. She had to admit that she did feel a little better from talking about things.

"So let me make sure I understand... you went to the hospital to visit her?" Dr. Bhatti asked.

Chrissie nodded. "Yes. It was weird and awkward, but I showed up. For whatever that was worth. My mom was so high on meds I don't know how much she'd even remember from that day."

"Sometimes people going through crises get impressions of others, even if they can't acknowledge them in conscious ways. I'm sure she appreciated your visit."

Chrissie scoffed. "My mother? Appreciate me? Florence Demata doesn't appreciate anyone but herself. She *tolerates* me. She might even... be abusive. I don't know. I don't know what a healthy relationship with a mother looks like, so I have no point of reference for what's normal, let alone healthy."

That got a nod from Cynthia.

"And why," Chrissie continued, "should I go out of my way to make *her* feel good? She barely even did the basics for me growing up. And forget about once I became in adult. Mother in name only. She doesn't deserve to get more than she gave me!"

"I understand. It's hard when our parents are incapable of being there for us in the way we want."

"A warm meal. A proper lunch. A fucking hug! She locked herself in her room with a bottle of wine when I was six years old and sick. Ridiculous! They should have requirements before women can become mothers."

"Your feelings are completely valid. But can you see that your mother is a woman with her own trauma and limitations?"

"Oh, she definitely has limitations. That doesn't matter. *I* didn't matter. Should I sell out my own needs on her behalf because she's *traumatized*?"

"No. Not at all Chrissie. It sounds like some serious boundary issues may have developed in your relationship with her. Maybe enmeshment."

"What is that?"

"Enmeshment refers to losing yourself to a needy parent. The emotional boundaries blur, and you can find yourself sacrificing your needs so your parent feels happy. Often it comes out of the desire for approval or love. It's a coping mechanism. But as we age, it becomes more and more of a nuisance that prevents us from developing fully and getting our needs met."

Chrissie shrugged. *Shit.*

"Does this sound familiar?"

"Maybe."

Cynthia pulled a book from her shelf behind her and leafed to a page marked with a Post-it Note. "This book here talks in detail about enmeshment. For example... do you feel like you've neglected your true needs for so long that you feel empty and unfulfilled? That's when you feel guilt and shame when separated from your parents, even though being with them can feel equally uncomfortable in other ways."

Chrissie nodded. "Yes. That resonates. I-I'm... just having trouble understanding what all this means."

"There's nothing to fear. It's safe. It's just a new way for you to understand your relationship with your mother. It can help you reframe your understanding of what's already happened so you can become whole."

"What does 'becoming whole' even mean? What does it look like?"

"That's a good question. It looks different to every person. It might look like setting boundaries with your mother... or learning to parent yourself so you're not seeking your mother's love."

"But I *deserve* my mother's love," Chrissie said, tearing up.

"You *do* deserve it. But... she can't give you love the way you want it. Knowing that, how will you move forward?"

"I don't know. It all feels so disappointing. Like I was deprived of some essential right I deserved as a little girl."

Dr. Bhatti shut her book and said, "Do you ever talk to your inner child?"

"I don't know that I've ever done that consciously."

"That's alright. We're going to try that now. I invite you to give your inner child permission to feel whatever it is they are feeling. Let's do an exercise right now. Place your feet firmly on the ground and close your eyes. Breathe in and out four times."

Chrissie did as she was told. *What do I have to lose?*

"Let me know when you've finished your four breaths."

Chrissie felt the air moving in and out of her. With each breath, the heaviness in her chest grew a little lighter. "Done."

Cynthia continued. "Now just imagine your inner child. Little Chrissie could be any age. Maybe four years old, or seven. Just allow your intuition to guide you." She paused for a time. "Are you in touch with your inner child?"

"Yes."

"Great. Ask her to tell you how she feels and what she wants most in this moment."

Chrissie listened. Her inner child was quite chatty. She'd probably been waiting a lifetime for Chrissie to listen to her and truly see her. Much like big Chrissie had been waiting her whole life for her mother to see her.

"Just take it all in," Cynthia said. "Listen completely. Let little Chrissie know that what she feels is all valid. It's all worthy. Then before you say goodbye—for now—ask her if there is anything she'd like you to do for her. Sometimes it's as simple as eat a favorite food, or visit a specific place. Just ask her what would make her feel better right now."

The moment fell silent as Chrissie communed with herself across time.

"Now take a deep breath and, when you're ready, open your eyes."

Chrissie opened her eyes and felt refreshed.

"Okay then," Cynthia said, her speech slow and warm. "Do you want to share your experience?"

Chrissie nodded. "It's kind of weird. My inner child was dressed in this bright-pink tutu, and she had a tiara on her head. She had a sort of sparkly wand with a star on the end. A magic wand of sorts, I guess."

"What did she want to tell you?"

"She was bored and upset that I hadn't checked in with her for so long. She wants us to do something totally focused on ourself instead of catering to someone else's needs. She also specifically requested pepperoni pizza for dinner from a cool spot near my apartment. She wants me to meet someone there and have fun."

Cynthia laughed. "Very specific. Great. Now the key is, you have to give her what she asked for so she knows you're listening. Those are your marching orders for today. Get a pepperoni pizza!"

"Well... if all therapy sessions end like this, sign me up!" Chrissie giggled awkwardly along with Cynthia.

Her therapist said, "There is one other thing I'd like you to do before our session next week. Please write in your journal. I'll email you a few prompts. And if FaceTime is easier than in-person, we can keep meeting this way. Same time and place next week?"

Chrissie nodded. She didn't feel horrible, so maybe she'd try this again.

She knew exactly where she was getting pizza from tonight: Rocco's Tavern on Main Street in Culver City. She sent Becky a text asking her to meet there around five, and she immediately replied that she'd be there.

Pizza and drinks was something she already considered herself an expert on. If therapy was all about feeding herself pizza, then Chrissie was definitely into therapy. She felt a sudden burst of lightness rise through the core of her pain. It was the spark of possibility. A new way to look at life.

She scanned her email. Cynthia had already sent her several journaling prompts, so Chrissie got out her journal and a pen and started writing.

The first task was to describe her core dilemma. She wrote, *My core dilemma is that I want my mother to really see me, love me, connect with me. I want her to tell me she loves me and provide support to me. I want to feel like I haven't been abandoned by the woman who is supposed to be my biggest supporter.*

Chrissie stopped as she felt her throat closing up. She'd rarely thought of the word "abandoned" in relation to her mother—but when she wrote it on the page, it rang true. Flo had always been emotionally unavailable, which made Chrissie feel rejected and abandoned. Such treatment made her believe she was not enough.

The next journal prompt asked, *What do you have a habit of doing?*

Chrissie wrote the first thing that came to mind. *I have a habit of absorbing myself into people and situations, accommodating others' needs, and morphing myself into what I think they need to the point that I don't even realize who I am any longer. How can any relationship last if it's not a partnership with give and take? Instead, I'm always in a muppet-versus-human-being situation. The muppet—being me—constantly looks to the other person for guidance as to who they are. Eventually the human being moves on and the muppet is stuck looking for another host to determine who they are and what they should be.*

Chrissie set her pen down and wiped her eyes on her sleeve, then continued. *I'm pathetic. This is why my marriage was guaranteed to fail. Because I never defined who I am or what I want. I spent the last five days being doe-eyed and accommodating a woman who never really does anything truly loving for me. Because I was looking for her to give me what I needed since I was young. Instead, I got the shaft. Again. I'm so stupid.*

She placed her journal on the coffee table.

Clearing out my true emotions is overwhelming. I don't know if I have the capacity for this.

She stared at the ceiling for a while, wishing she could tap away all the pain and frustration with Lil Chrissie's magic wand. Wading through a lifetime of torment was tedious. At least she had something fun to look forward to—it was nearly time for happy hour.

Chapter 5: Energy

Chrissie went to her closet to select a cute outfit. Sporting a ruffled red top, skinny jeans, and wedges, Chrissie walked down Culver Boulevard to Main Street. Inside the bar, she found a high-top table for two and settled her tushie into her seat. A text from Becky told her she would be there soon.

Chrissie ordered a St. Germain martini and boneless hot wings. She was sure her inner child would approve of anything bite-sized and dipped in ranch dressing.

Becky arrived. In an instance of lovely synchronicity, she too was wearing a red top—peplum style—with jeans. She ordered the same martini as Chrissie from the waitress before gushing, "How cute are we?"

"Very cute. Thanks for meeting me on short notice."

"Thank you? I was *desperate* for something to do, so thanks for saving me. The office is such a hot mess right now. I think Vanessa is getting worse without you around—she is so unprofessional! She's mentioned you, keeps saying out loud that you've abandoned your job. I think human resources should get her head on a platter. All she does is add negativity and drama to the office."

Chrissie chortled. "Sounds like my mother."

"How's that going, by the way?"

Chrissie's laughter died on her lips. "It's *not*. We had a huge fight. She basically manipulated me into staying at her house with some fake paperwork. I know she's manic-depressive, but this betrayal went beyond the pale."

Becky's jaw was hanging open.

Chrissie pursed her lips. "Sorry. I wasn't going to mention my mom's mental illness."

"No, I get it. Believe me. My brother was diagnosed with bipolar, and it's a challenge. I can't imagine growing up with a *mom* who had it. That must have been hard on you."

Chrissie felt herself tearing up again. Was this going to be her life? Crying over spilled milk endlessly? What would happen when she depleted the world's supply of mops?

"I'm sorry," Chrissie said. "It just happened this morning, and then I had my first ever call with a therapist. I feel a bit raw."

Becky leaned over with a sweet look and simply put her hand on Chrissie's. "That's what friends are for."

That made Chrissie even more teary-eyed. She wiped the corners of her eyes. How long had she avoided connecting with others? For a while now she'd felt like none of her friends really knew her true struggles and feelings. *My mantra has always been that I want to feel connected, but I don't want to get attached to anything or anyone. Attachment hurts. So does being alone.*

"What was it like when your brother was diagnosed?" Chrissie asked.

"It was awful. I mean, he's really smart. He was valedictorian at his high school. Then he went away to college—we're talking Harvard—and had a mental breakdown his first semester. They say people can have these dormant genes predisposing them to bipolar disorder, but that something has to trigger it. Ivy League schools put on a lot of pressure. We don't really know exactly what happened, but he ended up in the hospital in Boston. And, you know, here we were, all the way in Los Angeles, so we couldn't easily go visit him. My parents were dying with worry. So was I."

"Sheesh." Chrissie whistled. "I read a lot online about how to approach the illness. But it seems like you just have to be patient and accept the afflicted person's situation for what is. Not much that can really be done about it."

"Mhmm. My brother actively worked on his recovery and selected the best meds to help him stabilize. That seemed to help a lot. When he came back home after his first breakdown, he wasn't making total sense. He kept asking me to reread this poem on my bedroom wall. All the while he seemed to be in another world. I just wasn't connecting to my brother like before. It was like something had taken over him."

"Maybe that's how it was with my mom. I think rather than allowing me to see what was happening to her, she would hide in her room and hope it would go away. And this was over thirty years ago, so mental health wasn't as good as it is today. I'm... learning, now, that those moments made me feel unlovable, unworthy. No wonder my marriage failed. But I'm not sure how I feel about talk therapy."

"It has its uses. Maybe you can try to stick with it for a bit to help you work through some things? I've been finding more and more that energy healing seems to speed up the process and help clear things out faster than talking. Although it can take years to really feel like you've moved to a new place in your life."

Chrissie scoffed. "I feel like I don't have years. I'm getting old! I waited so fucking long to start looking at my issues that I've done myself a disservice. What if I die before I get better?"

"Forty isn't old anymore, girl!" Becky laughed. "Look at J-Lo! And better to start now than never. What if you went to the end of your life and never explored all these parts of yourself?"

Chrissie sighed. "You're so right. I never knew there was an emotional guru hiding in my company's accounting department all this time." Chrissie and Becky laughed together and sipped at their martinis. "So what's this energy work you're talking about?"

"Apparently there are a lot of modalities people use. Enough to make your head spin. But I've been seeing a reiki practitioner in Eagle Rock and it feels so soothing and helpful in my journey. Sometimes I feel when I talk too often about things that upset me, I just get more and more focused on the trauma emotions. Girl, you don't want to get stuck in your trauma. The goal is to move through the trauma and release it from your physical body and your aura."

"Whoa. That's right up my alley. It sounds cool."

"It's a constant process. I mean, not to scare you, but it becomes maintenance. Like, clearing your energy is weekly or even daily thing. Once you learn more about what works for you, you'll be able to take ownership, do some of your own clearing and sorting. You won't need a therapist in your face asking you questions like, 'Yo dawg, how does that make you feeeeel?'"

Chrissie laughed at Becky's therapist impression. "That sounds interesting. I mean, I sage my apartment regularly... smells good, but I don't feel like it helps me evolve."

"Maybe you've been using some of these tools with the hope they'd do the work for you? It's always easier to avoid the hard stuff, but you'll get so much stronger and enjoy your life more if you can muster the courage to face yourself."

"Hmm." Chrissie swirled the ice in her glass thoughtfully. "I hate to admit it, but you're probably right. I didn't even know how to start looking at the hard stuff. It terrifies me."

"You're already on your way. Start with feeling abandoned and unlovable and move through it until you can feel the opposite. Journaling is a great tool to get those thoughts and beliefs out of your head and heart and onto paper."

"Goodness, that sounds great. Send me the info for your Eagle Rock healer too."

"Definitely. Now, this shit can get heavy fast so I'd like to scarf down a wing and change the subject."

"Yes! New topic."

"I have a date Friday with a new guy."

"Whaaat? Tell me more about this date. Where are you meeting him?"

Becky elaborated on a man she'd met fortuitously at independent bookseller The Last Bookstore in downtown LA. She'd been reaching for a book by Carl Jung and lost her footing on the step stool. A man named Jason caught her mid-flight. After her nerves calmed down, they began discussing psychology, sound healing, and polarity therapy. They had an instant connection and he invited her to a sound bath followed by dinner.

Chrissie left the restaurant thinking that Becky really had her shit together. Chrissie had seen clairvoyants and psychics before, but she always felt like they took her money and nothing ever changed. Maybe they just told her what she wanted to hear? It was rare to look in the mirror and see where she needed to evolve, but she was certain Becky had done her a solid with her advice.

Chrissie felt very lucid about one thing: She did *not* want to wake up in ten or fifteen years and realize she was the same miserable, lost gal she'd been for most of her life. That would be so sad. Chrissie wanted her life to feel joyful, connected, and free. That meant she *had* to change.

Her phone pinged with a message from Moof. *Hey kiddo. Just checking in on you. Your mom told me you gals had a fight.*

Chrissie didn't respond. She had to process her own thoughts before she could decide whether to respond to him or not.

That night her head was swimming and she couldn't sleep in spite of—or because of?—the two martinis and glass of pinot grigio in her system. She got up at midnight, peed, then started writing in her journal about anything and everything that came to mind.

Would she ever talk to her mother again? Why did Flo have to be who she was? Why couldn't she be kind, empathic, and loving? Could she trust Moof? What should she do about returning to her job when the very thought of doing so made her skin crawl? Why couldn't she be more creative and find new ways to earn money? Could she trust Moof, or would he spy on her or manipulate her like Flo did?

She scrolled Instagram and found Becky had sent her the healer's info like she said she would. Chrissie clicked through and sent a note to the healer, Avril, requesting an appointment. She had plenty of time while away from work. *Why not plow through a lifetime of unearthed trauma?*

She finally got fed up with her insomnia and reached for a bottle of melatonin as well as some valerian root. Then she stared at the ceiling for a while, watching her incessant thoughts dance across the ceiling. Eventually, sleep took her.

Chrissie awoke to the sounds of birds chirping. Feeling refreshed, she lingered in bed for a little while, just enjoying the peaceful songs of the trouble-free creatures.

She prepared a fresh pot of coffee and checked her messages. Avril, the Eagle Rock healer, had responded that she had an opening today. That gave Chrissie purpose to her day and a distraction from her endless mental chatter about her mother. She enthusiastically accepted the open appointment.

A few hours later, she parked in front of Avril's house in a cute Eagle Rock neighborhood. The front yard was lusciously filled in with native plants blooming sprouts of white, purple, and bright-orange flowers. Soothing, slender tufts of lavender and fragrant sage framed the walkway to the front door. Lilac and gray flowers offered up a calming embrace that fortified Chrissie as she searched for the courage to face her fears.

Before she got to the door, she was greeted by the sound of little yipping dogs bombarding her at the entrance. She couldn't see them yet, but she most certainly could not miss their barks.

The door opened to a serenade of furry vocalists.

Mistress Avril stood in the doorway, adorned with a smile, her ears garnished with large wooden hoop earrings. Her hair was wrapped in a head scarf embellished with rhinestones and swirls of blue, purple, and bright-yellow silk. *Her scarf matches her garden!* Waves of smoky blond hair peeked out around the edges of the scarf and a few wispy gray strands framed her face. A single citrine-colored rhinestone decorated her third eye.

Wise and *stylish*, thought Chrissie, feeling impressed on the spot.

"Hi, Chrissie!" Avril's smile was big and genuine and bubbly, but not in the annoying way Chrissie found some people in Los Angeles could be. She was already convinced Avril was not fake-bubbly—she was the real deal. Avril gave Chrissie a warm, loving hug.

"Sorry about my fur babies. They're nuts. But they're also cute, so we keep them around." She smiled again. "Since it's such a beautiful day outside, I'd love for us to do your session today in my backyard. Is that okay for you?"

Chrissie nodded vigorously. "That sounds great. Maybe I could get a glass of cold water to help with the hot flashes?"

Chrissie felt she'd bungled the joke. Avril laughed anyway.

Avril filled a tall tumbler with ice and a wedge of lemon and poured water to the top. She didn't hand it to Chrissie, but instead escorted Chrissie to the yard as she played hostess with water glass in hand. She moved with precision and purpose, and Chrissie surmised that it was better to move quickly with her than get run over.

Two red Adirondack chairs flanked a raised garden bed that dominated the back half of the yard. A wooden spirit house stood perched on a tree stump. Avocados, figs, and lemons grew in abundance on the trees surrounding them. The chairs faced one another slightly at an angle and were shaded by an enormous black-and-white-striped umbrella.

Avril's dogs cheerfully waddled after them like a furry little support group. She introduced them to Chrissie. There was a black-and-white, short-haired Chihuahua named Truffle, a fluffy white poof ball named Marshmallow, and a little senior Yorkie called Grammy. Chrissie had not known herself to be a dog person, but at that moment she welcomed *all* the energetic support she could get.

Avril asked Chrissie to sit down in one of the chairs and close her eyes. "Here we go. Breathe through your feet and ground yourself," she coaxed as she waved a burning sage wand around Chrissie's head and at the base of her feet.

Avril set the sage wand on a blue, handmade ceramic bowl to let it smolder. An intricate stump of wood—per Avril, a family heirloom more than eighty years old—served as an outdoor table. It hosted a box of tissues that Chrissie suspected she would reach for sooner than later.

"Tell me: how I can help you today?"

"Well..." Chrissie exhaled slowly and said, "To make a long story short, my dad died when I was very young, and around that time my mom became mentally ill. She was eventually diagnosed with bipolar. Anyway, she became very neglectful and our relationship soured. We've been estranged on and off again for many years. I recently stayed with her after she had a mental breakdown. But then I found out she'd manipulated me into staying with her—she even forged medical documents to trick me—and then she seemed to turn on me. And I just lost it. Anyway, I'd love guidance on that relationship. And I'd like help being true to myself, instead of giving myself away to make others happy."

There was a silence that lingered. Chrissie looked up and caught a brief glance of Avril's face. Her expression seemed to say in no uncertain terms, *What the fuck kind of mess am I dealing with here?*

But Avril's voice exuded only confidence. "Let me take a look." She put her hands together in prayer and closed her eyes for what felt like quite a while. Chrissie watched as she did strange clearing motions with her hands. They appeared to be moving as if she was jiggering with the wiring behind the monstrous servers of a data center.

Finally, she took a big breath, in and out, then opened her eyes and spoke. "Your mantra... for quite a long time has been, 'Use me, abuse me, take me for granted.' Like the lyrics to a catchy song, except this isn't a song, it's your life. This mantra definitely stems from your relationship with your mother. As my own healer, Rev Zoe Inman, would say: 'It's your master wound.' You learned to subdue yourself to try to gain your mother's love and attention because you were so young, and her behavior felt so harsh. You originally did this as a protective mechanism. But this protective mechanism has stayed in place for so long that it's become twisted and almost cut off energy to your power center, your solar plexus!"

"Oh. My. God," Chrissie gasped. "Please tell me I won't be stuck like this forever!"

Avril smiled in sympathy. "Everything is malleable when we are ready to change and willing to do the work necessary. I was able to loosen that chokehold of old fear and abuse from your solar plexus, allowing you to breathe easier and begin to explore who you really are and what you want from this life. Take some time throughout this upcoming week to place your hand on your solar plexus and breathe into it. Repeat the mantra, 'I am a powerful and sovereign being.'"

Chrissie nodded in agreement.

"I was also able to clear a cord from your mother to you. It was taking up quite a bit of your stomach and heart areas. She may have been tapping into your life force and sucking it up for herself, which took away your identity and inhibited your natural courage. I let her know she is not allowed to cord you anymore! But you have to reinforce this. You must cut your cords and clear your aura routinely. This is all energetic, but very powerful. I'll send you a video that shows you how to do it yourself whenever you want. I also cleared your aura and filled the cracks with gold, like the Japanese practice of kintsugi."

Chrissie teared up in awe. "Thank you so much. I guess I'm unsure of what's next? I'm so new to this and it all feels so massive."

Avril nodded. "It's a lot to take in. Be gentle with yourself. Warm salt baths are always recommended. Light your favorite candles, surround yourself with beauty. The simple life force and beauty of a flower arrangement can also really support you. I have some of those for purchase, if you'd like."

Avril strode before Chrissie and raised her hands to the sky in splendor like a great Zerit Bird flying on the wind. "Remember that healing is a lifelong process, and as you go through it you will find moments when you feel totally free and full of joy. You'll look back and realize you are—and have—things you could only dream of before. But healing from your master wound—your mother and father wounds—will take time. Be patient with yourself. Find ways to parent yourself so that you feel loved and supported whenever you need it. Journaling can help. I also find it beneficial to write a letter to each parent to release all that pent-up emotion. You can burn the letter afterwards, outside of your home. Set your intention on releasing the old wounds, resentment, and trauma as the letters burn away."

Chrissie wiped her eyes. It was all too much. Why didn't they teach practical tools growing up, like how to heal your wounds, manage your emotions, and support your needs? Here she was, at the ripe age of forty, only just learning to take care of herself. She was almost embarrassed by her lack of understanding of how to heal. Shouldn't she know this stuff by now?

"Thank you," Chrissie said, careful not to show her embarrassment.

"You're very welcome."

Chrissie and Avril hugged. Avril's embrace felt motherly. Maybe Chrissie could find mother figures in other places instead of trying to force her mother to be what she wanted her to be.

"I also do phone sessions if you ever want support and don't have the time to drive out here."

In an effort to be gentle with herself, Chrissie treated herself to lunch in Eagle Rock before trekking through Los Angeles traffic back home. Gentle to her meant "gentle, healthy foods." She'd asked Avril for a recommendation and thus proceeded to Four Café, a restaurant that featured seasonal foods with a range of meat and vegetarian options. Chrissie felt the urge for something plant-based at that moment and ordered a curried chickpea sandwich with a side of soup. Its warmth would nourish her body.

She sat outside at a table underneath a tree and drank cold, fresh water, watching people walk up and down Colorado

Boulevard. She wondered if everyone else but her knew these secrets about healing and overcoming childhood trauma. After consecutive talks with Cynthia, Becky, and now Avril, it sure seemed that way.

Or did each person have to seek and find their path to the old beliefs in order to become a new person? Maybe Jesus dying on the cross and being resurrected was a metaphor for each human life? Maybe the old you did have to die before a new you could be born? After all, saying goodbye to an old version of yourself was painful and scary. Chrissie was only doing it because there was nowhere else to go. She was tired of beating her head bloody against the same wall and ending up in the same exact places, over and over and over again.

Pondering, she vaguely recalled a famous saying she'd once read from Anaïs Nin. Searching on her phone, she found the exact quote: *And the day came when the risk to remain tight in a bud was more painful than the risk it took to blossom.*

Chrissie lowered her phone and clutched at her heart. *This saying so succinctly summarizes this moment in my life.* She wasn't ready for change and had so much more to learn about growth and healing, but she just couldn't take being subjected to her mother's abuse anymore, being a willful and subservient participant in her own bondage. If she wanted to live beyond misery—to create a second chapter in her life—she had to find the path forward.

She slurped up the last spoonful of soup, a rich and soft butternut squash garnished with fresh herbs. She realized now that people could change, but only if their back was up against a wall. Was Flo capable of change? She shook her head wearily.

Putting too much stock into that wish could prove dangerous. She shooed that thought away before it could take root.

Feeling more whole than usual, she felt compelled to respond to Moof's text before heading home. *I don't know if I feel I can trust you fully. Me and my mom have a long history of challenges. Rather not discuss via text.*

And with that, she walked to her car and headed home.

The next morning, Chrissie awoke to a feeling of melancholy. Thrashing in her dreams, she recalled an image: it was her younger self—the little Chrissie she'd spoken with days ago—abandoned on an island and feeling totally alone. Chrissie had been deeply terrified of having to figure everything out without her mother to help.

She woke up in the grip of that despair—the despair of letting go of her mother. Maybe they didn't have a healthy relationship, but Chrissie was still frightened that if she let go of her strained relationship with her mother, everything would fall apart. She'd be like the young girl she had witnessed in her dream: completely alone, with no one to support her. That feeling terrified her. She thought, *As a child, someone else is expected to care for you. As an adult, if you don't play your cards right, you end up solely responsible for absolutely everything about yourself. Everything in your life.* Chrissie didn't feel like she'd ever be capable of such self-responsibility.

Ironically, she'd received a text from Moof: *I understand. I'm here if you ever need anything.*

Of course, who knew what his agenda was. Still, Chrissie replied *thank you* just in case.

Right after that, a text from her mother arrived.

Chrissie please call me.

That infuriated her. She deleted the message immediately to avoid responding with words she couldn't take back.

In response to her request for a short call, later that day she spoke with her therapist Cynthia. Hoping this would provide another chance to continue moving forward into a new way of being, Chrissie took the call.

"Hello," Cynthia said, "How are you today? How's everything going?"

"It's going."

"Have you talked to your mom since our last call?"

"No. But she texted me today just asking me to call her. I have not."

"Oh boy. She didn't give you much to go on, did she?"

"It's just like her to put the ball in my corner so that I go into frustrated-followed-by-guilty mode for ignoring her."

"So how are you going to change your response to her action?"

"I don't know. That's why I'm talking to you! I thought you'd offer something."

"Well, there is no magic pill for these things."

Chrissie rolled her eyes. What was the point of speaking to a professional if they didn't offer tips for a regular person like her?

"Don't worry, Chrissie, you're going to find out you have something better than magic pills, and it's already inside you. First, let's start with breathwork. Stop and take four long breaths in and out. Close your eyes if it helps you feel more comfortable. Let me know when you're done."

Chrissie gritted her teeth as she began. This was so frustrating. Couldn't she just blast all this negative crap out of her being and move on with her life?

But by the fourth breath, her jaw had gone lax and she was starting to feel somewhat open-minded. "I'm done."

"Now imagine you can talk to your mom without having to call her or go see her. Tell me exactly what you would tell her."

Chrissie sighed loudly and intoned, "I am tired of not having my emotional needs met by you and feeling manipulated by you. I don't want you to think that I don't care, but I also have to take care of myself first."

"Okay, good. How did that feel?"

"Okay. A small shift, like I was standing my ground instead of wilting. But I feel like I could never say what I just said to you directly to my mom. Or, even if I did, like she wouldn't honor it. She'd trample me."

"Trust your instincts. If it ever feels right to say those words to her, you will. But I think the idea we're after is going beyond your mother validating your needs. Unfortunately, you have a mother who can't do that for you, no matter how much you wish she would. Now, Chrissie, how can you tell that the boundaries and feelings you just expressed are valid?"

Chrissie paused, then said, "How I feel is enough. It has to be. I need to take care of my own needs. But it's so easy to backslide into negative thinking. How do I make this mindset stick and unhook from my unhealthy dynamic with my mom?"

"I think one step at a time is the best way to do it. When she triggers you, try to breathe four times before you respond. Journaling can also help you get all the anger and frustration out of your being and onto the page where it can't harm you. It might help to write a mantra on a Post-it Note and place it in several places around your house, or set it as a reminder on your phone. Something like 'my needs come before everyone else's' and 'I am allowed to set boundaries.'"

"Oh, oh. That's good." Maybe Cynthia was worth the trouble of seeing her after all. "Is doing this enough to change things?"

"It's a very good start. Small, conscious changes can have a big impact on your life. As you continue down this path, it will get easier. You'll be able to be communicate more clearly with your mother than ever before. And you can expand your growth into all of your relationships."

"Guess that means I need to think about what I really want and who I am."

"You got it. You get to focus on you now. You are the most important person in your life at this moment."

"That's pretty cool. But also scary."

"Yes, it can be. Try to approach the task creatively. Paint. Take a walk. Visit a garden or a museum. Doing so gives you a chance to think about things unconsciously without putting too much pressure on yourself. It's an exploration of your inner being. Instead of trying to actively figure it out, you allow 'the greatest expression of you' to take up space inside you. As you get out of your monkey brain, you can begin to listen to and honor your intuition."

Chrissie nodded along to Cynthia's words. A visit to a museum or garden sounded like a great way to spend her day. And if it helped her get a better sense of her own needs, well, then that was a bonus.

"Alright. I'll take that up as homework."

"Great. Same time next week?" Cynthia asked.

"Let's plan on it. Except... I have to decide if I'm returning to work next week or taking more time off."

"Got it. What is your instinct telling you?"

Chrissie thought for a moment, then said, "I'm leaning towards filing a formal HR complaint against my boss for abuse, and taking as long as I can to return."

Cynthia blinked quickly, processing the unorthodox response. Finally she said, "I'm glad you know what it is you want. Talk next week."

Chrissie hung up and leaned back against her couch, deep in thought.

The truth was, that was what she felt compelled to do. But she didn't know if such a plan was practical. It could backfire. If she stopped getting paid, her idea would go down in the trash heap of really bad ideas she'd implemented with gusto. But Becky had set her off. Ever since Becky had told her about The Griper's slanderous rantings while Chrissie was away from the office, she'd wanted to lodge a complaint and stop the abuse. It just wasn't right, and Chrissie didn't feel she could tolerate it any longer. Chrissie might not be a career gal, but she *did* deserve to be treated with respect at the office.

Beyond that, she also hoped to one day find enjoyment in her work. *One thing at a time, like Cynthia said*, she thought.

First, she needed to attend to her homework. She wanted to find a place to visit tomorrow to indulge in her creativity. She knew about Descanso Gardens near Pasadena and the Getty Center in Malibu. She was familiar with both, but neither felt like the right place to visit. She was, however, intrigued by the Japanese art of repairing broken pottery with gold and silver. Avril had mentioned kintsugi in their session. Chrissie wondered about Japanese museums or gardens nearby. After a quick search, it turned out there was a well-rated Japanese garden in Van Nuys. Van Nuys didn't always feel like a destination to write home about, but the garden itself looked beautiful in the pictures.

Chrissie reserved a ticket online and then moved on to her next adventure. She grabbed her purse and headed out to visit Michaels for art supplies. She had some ideas in mind. Instead of waiting for inspiration to find her, she decided to seek it out herself.

Michaels wasn't too crowded that afternoon, and Chrissie was grateful for that. She had a small budget in mind and wanted to take her time exploring all the craft supplies before picking her favorite items.

She loaded her cart with a beginner's painting set with oil paints and brushes along with a starter pack of canvases. Then she perused all the embellishments: rhinestones, beads, artwork, trinkets, stickers, and more. *Whoever came up with this store's theme was one heck of a creative person*, she thought appreciatively.

She picked up a couple of foam boards, a chalkboard easel that was just too cute to pass up, a selection of rhinestones and faux florals, and various essential items like chalk, glue, and scissors. There were so many cool items, and Chrissie was bursting with more childlike creative energy than ever before. Despite the splurge, the total at the register came close to her $80 budget. *This is easier than happy hour!*

She lugged her bags out to the car and headed home. There was a bottle of wine in the fridge, a frozen lasagna in the freezer, and bags full of craft supplies ready for her attention.

At home she put the Hallmark channel on the TV for background ambience, poured herself a nice glass of pinot noir, and put mixed nuts in a pretty bowl to have on hand for snacking.

She began at the dining room table with the small chalkboard she picked up at Michaels. On it she wrote, *I am worthy. I am the most important person right now*. She placed it on the side table next to a plant where she could see it from anywhere in her living or dining rooms.

Next, she pulled out one of the canvases and the paint set. After unwrapping everything, she started sketching on the canvas with her pencil, humming a happy tune to herself.

She squirted some paint colors onto a plastic paint tray and began creating her art. By the end, she was feeling really proud of herself. Just taking the time to enjoy something creative was so fulfilling. She'd been in a huge rut for years and hadn't truly realized it until now. She thought, *It's amazing what you can tolerate when it just festers underneath the surface of your life like a pimple that refuses to pop.*

Her first painting was an unintentional ode to Andy Warhol. It depicted a sprightly light-yellow jar with the word "Vaseline" scrawled across it. Beneath that was the phrase, *Life is a Journey. Bring Lube.*

That made her chuckle from her own cleverness. She'd found a creative outlet for her snarky personality. She had a couple more ideas for paintings like this one. Could she use the art to create a snarky and tough love set of tarot cards?

That would be the ticket! Instead of fluffy positive memes and clichéd phrases, she could offer something with true insight about life's challenges, sprinkled with a wicked sense of humor. Thinking about it brought a huge smile to Chrissie's face.

She didn't know how to develop a set of tarot cards from scratch, but she could find out. For now, she was immersed in a feeling she hadn't felt in forever—feeling joyful in the moment.

She poured herself another glass of wine, turned the volume up on the Hallmark channel, and relaxed.

Later she napped on her couch and woke up feeling a bit fuzzy. Her phone was strobing. She had several missed several calls from Moof. His voicemail said, "Hey kiddo. I'm at your mother's house. She had a little fall and was upset. She seems okay now, but she keeps asking for you. I'm sorry if I'm crossing a boundary, but I just don't know what else to do besides contact you."

Geez. She fell? I doubt she'd have Moof lie about that on her behalf. What do I do? Crap.

She stretched her shoulders back and moved her neck side to side, trying to relax herself, then shook her head in dismay. She knew what she was about to do, but it felt like two steps backward into the old Chrissie she'd just shed.

She took a deep breath. She remembered what Cynthia had told her. *Take four deep breaths, in and out.* Chrissie situated her feet firmly on the carpet and closed her eyes while breathing in and out for four slow counts.

The breath revitalized her and stilled her anxiety.

Despite her calm, the decision was still the same. Maybe she needed closure? Maybe she needed to tell her mom a stern "no" to her face? Regardless, she felt like her instinct was guiding her to go.

She packed a small duffel bag, stuffing a change of clothes and some essential toiletries into it, just in case. She switched into a cozy but versatile sweatsuit in a cute shade of pink, scrawled with the word *JUICY* across the bum.

Was she crazy? She was actually going right back into the line of fire after just getting out. And it was too late at night to call one of her backups, Cynthia or Avril, for support. She shot an email to Avril with the details of what was about to go down and mentioned she might need a phone session tomorrow. Knowing she had people now that would support her was one of the pillars of the new Chrissie—*and I shouldn't push away valuable support. I have to pay for that support, but at least Avril's sessions are effective, soothing, and reasonably priced. Huh. That sounded like an ad for Marshalls. Or worse, a laxative.*

Giggling at herself, she texted Moof: *I'm on my way. Not sure how I feel about this.*

He replied: *Got it, kiddo.*

She took the duffel bag and grabbed an emergency bottle of wine in case this turned into an all-nighter. She prayed that the traffic had died down already. *Fingers crossed.*

The traffic was light as she dashed across the dimming hills under a setting sun. Her mind jumped from thought to thought. What did the future hold for her? What would become of her mother? What should she do about work?

Eventually, she exited the freeway. Her stomach dropped as her body confirmed she was entering a zone she didn't feel safe occupying. She kept breathing into her belly and reminding herself that she was strong. *I don't have to do anything that feels too uncomfortable.*

She parked her car and Moof was right outside the front door, pacing back and forth a short distance away. He gave Chrissie a nervous wave when he saw her.

He was out of breath as he said, "Sorry, kid. I know this is awkward, and I imagine you're not sure you can trust Flo right now. But she was almost hysterical about needing to see you. I wasn't sure what else to do but call you."

Chrissie pursed her lips. The universe had a mighty sense of humor, it sure did.

Moof opened the front door for her and pointed towards Flo's bedroom. She immediately knocked on her mother's door and entered slowly, ensuring no items were being thrown her way or heads spinning about like Linda Blair in *The Exorcist.*

Flo was hazy-minded. She moved her hand up slightly from the bed cover where she lay. There was an envelope next to her with Chrissie's name on it.

Chrissie warily sat on the edge of the bed. "I hope you're okay, Flo. I came because Moof asked me to, but I won't be coming around much anymore. Might not answer the phone or respond when you call, either. It's time for me to focus on myself now."

Flo nodded as if she understood. She lightly tapped the envelope.

Chrissie took hold of it. She'd open it later.

She placed her hand on Flo's and lightly caressed her. "I'm not ready to love you. I'm not sure I'm ready to forgive you. I just want to stop blaming you and holding myself back for what you couldn't be. You weren't the mother I wanted and needed, but you *are* my mother."

Chrissie walked out of the room, softly closed the door, and then bolted through the front door into the fresh air. She flung her head down to her hands and cried. *Why does life have to be so fucking hard!* She wiped her eyes and opened the envelope. Inside was a simple note.

"I'm sorry. I love you. -Flo."

Folded within the plain white paper was a crystal clear photo of Chrissie with her dad. It was the day she'd gotten an A in her English class, and he'd told her how proud he was. Chrissie was in a dorky, overblown pink satin dress and polished black Mary Jane shoes. It was a clear photo of Giovanni, the first she could remember seeing his face. Her emotions were all over the place at this moment.

She clasped the photo to her chest and breathed a sigh of relief. She had a living memory of her dad. She could picture him now. Clearly see him. His chiseled jaw and warm smile that always made her feel welcome.

"Thank you, Mom," she whispered.

Moof peeked his head out the front door. "Are you okay?"

"I don't know. What is okay, after all?"

"Do you want to chat?"

"Mmm. Maybe just sit in silence for a few moments. But not inside the house, please."

"How about over there." He pointed to two chairs and small table near the side garden.

Chrissie nodded. Moof grabbed his cane and stumbled a bit walking to the chair. "Are you alright?" she asked.

"Ah, it's fine. It's just my diabetic neuropathy acting up. Foot feels a bit weird. No biggie."

Chrissie nodded, even though she was pretty sure he was downplaying a more serious situation than he was letting on. She didn't want to pry. She didn't even have the energy to try.

Moof nodded at the photo she held in her hands.

"My dad," Chrissie said. "Giovanni. This is the first clear photo I've seen of him since she lit them all on fire after he died."

"Wow, kiddo. That's a big deal. I was so close to my dad. I would have been pretty sad if I didn't have any photos to remember him by."

"Almost thirty-five fucking years," she gasped. She clasped the image close to her chest again, afraid to let go of it.

Moof gave her a moment of silence. "Have you figured out yet, what you'll do next?"

Chrissie nodded. "I'm going to do something I haven't done in a long while. Focus completely on my own needs."

"Good for you, kiddo. Good for you."

They sat outside for a while without saying another word. Crickets hummed and birds chirped as the air cooled their skin.

Finally Chrissie whispered, "I'm so tired."

"Family stuff can be exhausting," Moof agreed.

Chrissie's mood perked a bit. "I started painting today. It was really fun."

"Wow! An artist in the family. A-ha! Are you going to hold an exhibit some day?"

She shook her head. "I doubt that. I don't know if people would get me. My stuff feels more like a rudimentary Warhol. It's meant to be sarcastic and humorous."

"Impressive."

Chrissie pulled out her phone and showed off the picture of her first painting.

When Moof finally finished laughing, he tapped her knee briefly. "I haven't had a laugh like that in a good long while. That's good. Really good! I know I could use some Vaseline for *my* life, a-ha!"

Feeling enthusiastic, Chrissie rambled, "And I have a lot of ideas for more paintings. I've been thinking of an onion unfolding with the caption 'How many freaking layers?' for therapy and healing. Or a spoof on the Hanged Man card, with a lady woman swinging upside down from a tree branch with a glass of wine right-side-up in one hand and a selenite wand in the other. Don't know the caption yet for that one."

"This is sounding like a full project! What are you going to do with these, kiddo?"

"I've never done it before, but I was thinking I could create what I'm calling 'Tough Love tarot cards.' Cards that are wickedly funny and give honest help to people. I'm hoping to encourage people to think for themselves and trust their intuition."

"A-ha! Fantastic. Invite me to your launch party. I might be in a wheelchair, but I'll still be rooting for you."

Moof really was an unexpected yet sincere cheerleader for others. She could just see him now in an oversized skirt with pom-poms, beaming like a proud parent in the back of the room.

"Thanks. It's just an idea right now."

"It's a really good idea. Don't talk yourself out of it."

"You got it. Hmm..." Chrissie glanced through the window into her mom's dark house. "I should go. Staying over with her tonight won't be good for me."

"I understand."

"You'll keep an eye on her?"

"Yep. I'll do my best."

Chrissie patted him on the back and got in her car. Her mixture of emotions overcame her. Would her mother ever be okay? Would Chrissie ever be back at the house on good terms? What came next?

Whatever happened, she knew she was going to do the best she could to preserve her life. No—she was going to go further. She'd rip the fabric of her existence open into something it had never been allowed to be during the decades she'd held her breath waiting for her mom to become someone she couldn't be.

What Chrissie wanted from a mother, Flo could not provide. Chrissie was sad and disappointed with this fact. But now she was free to live her life.

At home, she placed the sacred photo of her dad in a frame and hung it on the wall. Then she poured herself more wine and started on another canvas. She was too wired to go to bed. All of the newly awakened insights about her life were buzzing around inside of her. She felt like her DNA was rearranging itself to make room for a new version of Chrissie.

She wasn't sure how else to shake out all this excess energy—if anything, the longer she painted, the more buzzed she became. *I mean, I stood up to my mother!* It had been the first time in her life she'd felt truly clear and resolute. What a revelation!

All this time, Chrissie had been clinging to Flo in an energetic sense, saying, "Mommy, love me, please love me, Mommy. I can't live without your love." Her life had been a non-starter, stuck at a train station waiting for a mother's love that would never arrive.

What a damn relief to not be waiting anymore.

She kept her phone on silent and savored sleeping in. She'd planned to visit the Japanese gardens today, but after driving to the valley last night she did not feel like heading out there again today.

It was midweek, and all she could think of was her desperate craving for brunch. She was thinking of returning to City Tavern. Would she feel safe there? Why not reclaim that part of her life too? She seemed to be having great success in that arena these days.

She had an email from Avril, a response to her frantic email to her last night. Avril had wished Chrissie the best and hoped it all went well with her visit to Flo. Chrissie appreciated the kind words. It was nice to touch base with someone who seemed to have her honest best interest at heart, without manipulation or other agendas. She replied that she was okay and had stood her ground. It felt good to write her feelings down. They felt even more real.

Chrissie put on a flowy, cozy cotton dress and sandals. Feeling deserving of a treat, she called an Uber so she could avoid driving. Her ride dropped her off right in front of the restaurant and she ambled up to grab a seat on the patio.

She enjoyed people-watching as she sipped a cocktail at noon. It was amazing. She ate shrimp tacos and soaked up the sun.

She glanced at her phone and saw she had an email from her company's human resources department. They couldn't verify the doctor listed on the paperwork she'd sent—*Quelle surprise!* she thought. *Me too!* She'd only be able to take sick time for this week. Next week would be unpaid. What did she want to do?

Her perfect day had been interrupted, but she wouldn't let this email ruin it. She decided against calling work and instead sent an email reply.

I'm sorry to hear the paperwork can't be verified with the doctor. Are there any alternatives to allow me to use vacation time for next week? Also, I've heard through co-workers that my boss, Vanessa Kriper, has been denigrating me behind my back. She'd been abusive and rude towards me every day at work. I'd like to file a formal complaint against her.

Firing that off, Chrissie felt riled up and empowered. She texted Becky to let her know she'd lit a fire.

Yes! Someone needs to stand up to her antics, Becky replied.

It didn't feel like the practical decision, but Chrissie believed strongly that she should not return to that workplace and continue the same old charade. She had no idea how this would work out. If it didn't go her way, then she had a little savings and could probably collect unemployment.

She'd dunked two cocktails and was buzzing pretty hard. She asked for her check.

"No charge, ma'am," the waiter said. "The bartender remembers you had an incident here recently. We just want you to keep coming back."

Chrissie was wild with delight. That was one of the *coolest* things that had ever happened to her. She dug into her wallet and, fishing out her remaining cash, she handed the waiter a five-dollar bill. "For your tip, at least. And thank you so much."

She wondered if the bartender was merely a Good Samaritan looking over her, or possibly a secret admirer. She'd have to sit at the bar next time to find out.

She sent a text to Moof: *I don't want to go back to my job.*

Chrissie found she enjoyed having conversations with Moof. Her initial skepticism had been misguided. He was a good listener. You could throw anything at him and he'd just tap it back at you, like a game of Ping-Pong. How could he be so nice without demanding something in return? What was in it for him?

Do you have options? he replied.

Kind of. Can you talk?

Yup.

She connected her headset and dialed his number.

"A-ha! Hey, kiddo. How are you?"

"I'm pretty good. I just knocked back two cocktails while sitting on the patio of a restaurant in Culver City."

"Sweet. Enjoying your time off?"

"Yes. Unfortunately, my company can't verify the info from the doctor since my mom faked it, so I may have to go back to work sooner than later. But I just have this sense of dread about the whole thing. My boss is so rude and abusive, and I want to be so much more than just a mindless drone."

"Can you afford to take some time off to figure it out?"

"That's a great question and I've been thinking about it. I can't take forever off, but with unemployment and my savings I might get away with a few months. I could take a class and try some new things. Maybe even talk to a coach to help me figure out what's next."

"It sounds like you have a lot figured out."

"I... didn't think I did until I rattled off all those items to you. Huh, how about that? Having someone to listen to me say things out loud really helps. Moof, I've been wondering... Why do you have so much patience to listen to others?"

"Well, I wanted to be a priest because I enjoyed hearing others air their grievances. Although I didn't end up at the seminary, I've found many people I enjoy being friends with appreciate my gift for listening. And I'm glad to have the time to do it."

"Well, thanks for sharing your gift with me."

"A-ha! I'm happy to. What's next on your agenda?"

"Maybe a quick walk around town for some window shopping, and then it might be naptime."

"Sounds like a great plan. Enjoy yourself."

"Thanks, you too. Talk to you later."

She wondered if Avril could do energy healing on her career. She emailed her asking for a phone appointment. The urge to change her work path was hovering around her like a swarm of bees—incapable of being ignored. Something in the universe wanted her to move forward in a different way and it felt like it wasn't going to let up until she found a new path.

After wandering around Main Street in Culver City and popping into Trader Joe's for a bag full of wine and prepared meals, she headed home. By the time her Uber dropped her off in front of her house, she was almost falling asleep even though it had been a short ride. She was looking forward to an evening of journaling, painting, and watching movies with a full wine glass nearby.

Avril had texted her saying she had a last-minute cancellation that had opened up availability in thirty minutes' time, if she wanted to jump on a call. *The universe* really *has a sense of urgency about this whole thing*, Chrissie thought.

Yes, she replied.

She put away her groceries, then made herself a cup of green tea to help her wake up. She jotted down a few notes in her journal to share with Avril in their session.

- Career — new path, way forward, security
- Mother — releasing codependence, keeping boundaries

By the time Avril called her on Zoom, she was ready.

"Hi, Chrissie."

"Hi, Avril. Thanks for making the time to talk with me today."

"Sure. The cancellation happened last-minute, and I remembered you mentioning being off work for a week or two. What do you want to focus on today?"

"I guess two things. I've been thinking a lot about my job and how much I dislike it. My boss is abusive and I took matters into my own hands by emailing human resources that I wanted to file a formal complaint, but I don't quite know what'll come next. And then with my mom—the other night when I messaged you, I went over and stood my ground. I didn't stay there. I took a letter from her, then I ran. I was scared I wouldn't be able to continue to stand my ground and maintain healthy boundaries with her."

"What was in her letter?"

"A short note. And she gave me the first photo of me and my father I've ever had."

"Hmm. That's a big deal, right?"

"Yeah. After he died, she lost it and got rid of all our photos of him. I almost couldn't remember what his face looked like until I saw that photo last night." Chrissie started crying.

"Wow. This photo has a lot of meaning for you."

"It does. So like... can you help me?"

"Sure. Let's start with your parents first. Close your eyes and breathe out through your feet. Breathe through your feet sinking them into the earth. Imagine a sturdy, grounded earth energy returns back to you through your root chakra, and cascades through your entire body. You are grounded in the here and now, no matter what happens."

"I want you to picture your inner child. She might be around six or seven years old. She's stuck somewhere and we need to free her. Once we let her free, you can never, ever go back to that place again. Is that understood?"

"Yes. I understand," said Chrissie, keeping her eyes closed.

"Let me know when you've located little Chrissie."

Chrissie felt her breath move through her body as she plumbed the depths of her subconscious. "I see her. She's stuck in my childhood bedroom. She's hiding from her mom."

"We're going to help her escape. Explain to her why she needs to go with you. She needs to live a better life, a life where she has control and the freedom to exist as she wishes. Remind her that once she leaves, she can never look back. Let me know when you're done and she's free."

Chrissie nodded. She took little Chrissie's hand and spoke to her silently. *We have to go. We've been in this place for far too long. We no longer need to stay stuck here, hiding from Mom, hoping that Dad will come back. It's time for us to explore the big world outside and do some new things with our life. We're going to explore our creativity. We're going to have a reason to exist. Are you ready to leave?*

Little Chrissie looked at her dolls and took in the static memory of a room, realizing it was a sad, lonely place she had built to protect herself. There was nothing there for her anymore. She nodded in agreement and clenched little Chrissie's hand. *I'm ready.*

We're going to leave this room, exit the front door of Flo's house, and walk away and never look back, okay? No matter how hard it feels at times, we want to fully live our life. No more being stuck. Okay?

Little Chrissie shook her head up and down vigorously. She was ready for *more.*

They held hands and burst through the bedroom door and stormed out the front into freedom. A bright blue sky surged overhead. They breathed in deeply and hugged each other.

Chrissie began to cry. So much relief washed over her. She opened her eyes and Avril appeared, her hands clasped in prayer and eyes closed, honoring the moment.

"She's free. *We* are free."

"Congratulations. You have your whole life ahead of you now. It's what you make of it. Do you still want to touch on your career?"

After what she'd just gone through, was she ready for another revelation? Chrissie breathed deeply, in and out, centering herself. "Yes. Maybe just some guidance to help me."

"OK. I'll pull some cards for your career."

Avril placed the deck in clear sight so Chrissie could watch her cut the deck and pulled two cards. She held one up so Chrissie could see. "The first one is 'the Jester.' It represents the present situation, and intuition. You need to make a decision, but in order to do so you need to trust your intuition. The Jester guides you to assess the situation logically while also requiring you to trust your heart and take a leap of faith into the unknown."

Avril looked up from the deck to check on Chrissie.

Chrissie nodded. "This makes sense. It feels right. I don't want to stay at my job, but I'm afraid to leave."

"Take some time to write down how you want to feel in your next role. What's most important to you? Is it feeling valued, being creative, or an opportunity for growth? Get clear on that from your heart's perspective. Then I think your intuition will guide you."

Chrissie murmured in agreement.

Avril held up the other card. "Your second card is about your future career. It's the '10 of Water' card featuring a happy Buddha on the cover. It signifies harmony in relationships. The culmination of what we wish for, the joy and success in partnerships. It's a really auspicious card! I think if you get clear on what you want and stay persistent, you can really move into work that feels more fulfilling and successful."

Chrissie held her hands in prayer and nodded to Avril. "Thank you *so* much for your help. I'm going to work on the list of things I want in my next job the moment I hang up with you."

"Good. And it's my pleasure. Remember, Chrissie, be gentle with yourself. Salt baths and rest are always a good idea."

Chrissie smiled. They waved goodbye.

She got out her journal and wrote at the top of the page, *List of what I want in my next job.*

She paused to check Instagram. One of her favorite advocates of self-healing had posted, *When you grow up with chaos and uncertainty, a part of you seeks that out in your relationships. That's because it offers up a satisfying buzz of familiarity, even though it's detrimental to our mental health. By recognizing the patterns, you can change your relationship dynamics at home and in the workplace.*

Chrissie found this insightful. As she wrote more in her journal, she realized her workplace mimicked her personal life. Little Chrissie had been stuck in her childhood room, hoping for better days to come but staying in a very small personal space to avoid conflict and confrontation. At the office, she'd attracted a boss that treated her like trash when she wasn't acting like she was invisible, much like her mom had growing up. Big Chrissie had been stuck in a tiny cubicle at work, lacking confidence and avoiding taking up too much space. Wanting to be visible and recognized but afraid of being seen. It was time to change this dynamic.

She wondered if she should just cut ties between herself and the company and her boss. One clean, quick severance. She got out the video that Avril had sent, which guided people on how to cut cords. She plugged in her headset and started the video. She began by grounding, sending another cord from her root chakra down to the earth. Then she visualized her relationship with her company—Marcus, Shilling, and Rosenbaum. She didn't sense any ill will but felt that the company had existed as a holding space for her while she figured things out. She thanked it for being there for her and then cut the cord between her solar plexus and the company using gilded scissors. She was ushering in a new era for her life where she could feel confident, seen, and in control of her work.

Then she imagined her boss, Vanessa. The Griper. Thinking of her made her skin crawl. She didn't get any visuals, but had the sense that they had been corded many times before in many lifetimes in manipulative, unhealthy relationships. This was a big one. She steeled herself and dug her heels farther into the floor for grounding.

She spoke a command out loud. "It's time to end this manipulative and abusive relationship. You are no longer welcome to cord me or be a part of my being or my journey in any way ever again. This is goodbye." She took out her imaginary machete and hacked away at the multiple cords in her lower chakra that had bound her and Vanessa.

"Good riddance to you. I no longer allow you to abuse me."

She let out a huge sigh of relief. *What a burden to be carrying patterns that you didn't know you had*, Chrissie thought. *And what grand liberation to finally see clearly and be able to garner your own freedom. You go, girl!*

All this time, Chrissie had held the key to her own freedom. All she had to do was believe she was worthy of more and find the tools to help her take it.

She decided to take a salt bath and light some candles to honor all her recent breakthroughs. She'd let the warm water soothe away her former wounds and emerge phoenix-like as her new self. She lit the candles—*no self-immolation today, thank you*, she thought—and poured two cups of Epsom salt into the bath, then added a few droplets of rose essential oil.

She immersed herself up to her shoulders in the tub, sprinkling her head and third eye with saltwater. Zoning out, she stared at the flickering candle flame and enjoyed the soothing warm water on her shoulders and back. She remained in the bath until her feet were warm and pulsing, pruney wrinkles forming around each toe.

After she exited the tub and dried off, she rubbed each foot and massaged her shoulders with soothing lavender CBD lotion. She applied serum to her face and a dab of Balance essential oil on her temples to keep the mood going.

She put on her robe, then turned on the TV, searching for a movie to watch. She felt beyond relaxed, like a piece of goo oozing into her couch. *This is peak living*, Chrissie thought through heavy eyelids. Healing and releasing old stuff was as exhausting as it was exhilarating.

Chapter 6: Courage

Her phone pinged, waking her from imminent slumber. Christine Chan from her company's human resources department had left her a voice message and sent an email. In order to pursue any formal complaint against her boss, she'd have to come into the office to answer questions from HR and fill out paperwork.

Ugh. All the relaxation drained from her body in an instant as she imagined having to actually *go into* the office and possibly have a run-in with Vanessa. What would she say to her?

Just thinking about it made her head hurt. She decided to call Christine back and talk to her. Maybe there was some alternative? She hit reply and felt her chest tense further with every ring of the phone.

The dial tone clicked. "This is Christine."

"Hi, Christine. It's Chrissie Demata."

"Hi, Chrissie. You must have gotten my voicemail. Can you come in tomorrow? Sorting this out won't take much longer than thirty minutes."

"See, um... I'm really uncomfortable with the idea of coming in. Is there any other way we can do this?"

"I understand your discomfort. In order to file a formal complaint against a manager, we need to conduct a short interview with you and have you fill out and sign a form. This must be done in-person so we can notarize it. I know, this situation is stressful. But you should know, you are not the only one to make a complaint of this sort involving the person in question. It would be in your best interests—and very courageous of you—to speak up."

At Christine's words, Chrissie's heart skipped a beat. *I wasn't the only one?* Still, she sighed and remained silent. Her head was spinning, her insides churned—she felt everything *but* courageous.

"Chrissie, are you there? If you can come into tomorrow at eleven a.m., then I'll handle your interview personally. You can leave before lunchtime and get on with your day."

Begrudgingly, Chrissie agreed. "Okay."

"Thank you, Chrissie. I'll see you tomorrow."

The phone clicked. Chrissie felt sick. She wasn't sure what would be better for the anxiety. A glass of wine, or a Xanax? Or washing a Xanax down with a glass of wine. That was a winner, she knew. It wouldn't be the first time.

She could barely stand living in her own body at that moment. Her heart pulsed heavily from overwhelming anxiety.

Before she could act rashly, Chrissie changed her plan. Instead of immediately reaching for the bottle, she grabbed a canvas and started sketching with furious intensity. It felt like she was cursing Vanessa out with every stroke of her pencil. *Bitch, bitch, bitch, bitch, bitch!*

She painted in a scarecrow likeness of Vanessa with a plain black bun and a boring navy-blue suit jacket. In one hand the caricature held a stick, in the other a carrot. A sign next to her began to take shape as she painted and contoured the colors. It read, "I'm the boss bitch." Chrissie used red paint to cross out the "boss" reference—really, Vanessa was just a bitch. When she was done, she venomously barked, "Fuck you!" at the painting, then put it in the corner of the room out of view from where she watched TV.

That cathartic act had helped somewhat, but her nerves were still shot, so she listened to several reiki healing videos on YouTube that helped cleanse her aura and strengthen her courage. After everything, all that was left to do was inhale a portion of cheesy lasagna and wash it down with a glass of cabernet.

She polished off the bottle while watching a romantic flick on the Hallmark channel. Of course, the couple came together in the end and decided to run the countryside inn together while living happily ever after. Normally Chrissie would have scoffed at such fairytales, but tonight she enjoyed the sentimental wrap-up at the end. She just wished real life were so clean.

Real life—real relationships—were complex, messy affairs.

Chrissie struggled to find the right outfit to wear for her formal human resources complaint interview. She didn't want to come across as trying too hard in a black suit with a white top, nor did she want to look too casual in culottes and flats. After dumping a third of her wardrobe on the floor, she finally selected a pair of black-and-white chevron-print stretch slacks that were very stylish yet cozy. She paired it with a black peplum top—also comfortable—and a long strand of pearls to impart that she was taking this seriously. Comfy wedges with black-and-white detailing rounded out her look.

She was nervous. No coffee for her this morning. Better to be tired than wired with a nervous stomach. She was beginning to feel more concerned about this than her mother, and together her concerns were tipping her over the edge. But she *had* to do this. Maybe she would resign from her job? Or maybe she would take stress leave to give her more time to think about her next move? If she ran out of money, she could always cash out some of her 401k. Anything to avoid the discomfort of doing something she hated for someone who mistreated her.

She grabbed her purse and went down to her car, all the while nervously imagining what she would say to Vanessa if she ran into her. Chrissie had to protect herself and avoid a direct confrontation with her. Chrissie didn't want to make it look like *she* was the problem. She might have been a bit unenthusiastic about the job, yes. But a cruel person that made others' lives worse she was not.

Crap! What if the news leaks into the office gossip?

Stopping her car abruptly in the parking lot, Chrissie texted Becky to give her a heads up. *Don't say anything to anyone else about what's going down. I want you to know I'm still employed. Whether I'll stay there or not, I don't know yet.*

Becky's reply came instantly. She agreed she was sworn to secrecy and wished her luck.

Chrissie arrived at the corporate parking lot and decided to park in a different spot than usual. It was the least she could do to depart from the pattern of her old life. She took a deep breath, pushed her shoulders back, and steeled her confidence for the task at hand.

Instead of waiting in the lobby for Christine to come get her, Chrissie called her direct number while sitting in her car. She went to voicemail. *Dammit.* She would be late if she didn't go inside now.

She did her best to exude confidence as she strutted towards the main entrance. All the while her stomach did somersaults and her shoulders tensed.

She pushed the atrium door open and Kim the receptionist recognized her immediately.

"Hi, Chrissie. Returning to work?"

"Actually, not yet. I'm here to meet with Christine. She's expecting me. We have an eleven a.m. appointment."

Chrissie could tell Kim was curious about the details. Was Chrissie getting fired? Turning in her resignation? She guessed it would just add fire to the office gossip about her. But there was nothing she could do about that. She was trying to live her life and take care of her business. *Let them think what they want.*

She tapped her foot nervously as she stood. Kim offered for her to take a seat, but she was too antsy to sit down. She stared blankly through the windows, waiting for Christine to come get her.

Finally, Christine came through the main office doors. Nodding at Chrissie, she buzzed them through, taking her down the hall to her office. When they arrived, she closed the door and gave Chrissie a thoughtful, kind smile.

"Thank you for coming, Chrissie. I know this must be difficult for you with your mother being ill and all. Can you start by telling me about any specific incidents you had with Vanessa Kriper?"

Chrissie took a deep breath. *This is it.* "I don't know if being unkind is a violation of company policy. But lately I've had a lot of time to think, and two things have stood out to me. Once, when I first started working here and didn't know how to access the system, she called me an idiot out loud in front of my co-workers. At the time I was new and wanted to keep my job, so I said nothing. Another time much more recently, she gave me the wrong files to include in a presentation. When I pointed out that I used the file she'd given me, she blamed me and threw the jump drive at me. I don't think she did it on purpose, but her temper is *nasty* and it comes across as uncooperative. Now that I think about it... I can't confirm this, but my friend who works in another department says Ms. Kriper has been vocal about me during my time away. Saying things like I'm abandoning my job. Basically trash-talking me publicly in front of my peers."

As Chrissie spoke, Christine took furious notes and checked a few boxes on her online forms.

Chrissie continued, "I think the hardest part for me is finding the motivation to go to a job every day where the person I work for brings negativity and combativeness to every moment of my day. It really is a worst-case scenario for me. And honestly..." Chrissie hesitated for a second. "Honestly, I'm not sure I want to come back to my job. It's so unfulfilling and I've thought about taking stress leave. I just don't know how to proceed."

Christine looked up at her. "I understand. Thank you for sharing. Stress leave is an option that you can use for up to three weeks, but we would need a note from a doctor to validate that. You can send it to my attention if you decide to do that. Work shouldn't be the worst place to spend your time, especially if you're in the office eight hours a day. If you can have your doctor fill out these forms and sign the last page, I'll submit your claim to the legal department and let you know how the company decides to proceed."

Chrissie pursed her lips. There wasn't an immediate resolution to be had. Not yet. But at least she'd found the courage to speak up for herself.

She took the forms from Christine and stood up. "Thank you for listening."

Christine nodded and escorted her down the hall, where—of all *freaking* luck—Vanessa Kriper was walking at that exact moment. Vanessa's stare felt dark and judgmental.

Christine spoke up, saying curtly, "Please wait for me outside my office, Vanessa. I'll be with you shortly." As she led Chrissie into the main lobby, she said, "I'm sorry about that. She wasn't supposed to arrive until later today. I'll be in touch."

Chrissie nodded and headed out to her car. When she opened the door she collapsed into her seat. He legs wobbled about like noodles. *Phew! I made it through.*

Becky sent her a text that called her a "rockstar." It felt good to have support. She wasn't sure how all this would shake out, but she felt good for doing it. Now that today's hard exercise was done, what to do next? Something fun for sure, which was why Moof's incoming text stood out as excellent timing.

Hey kiddo. Heading out to the Westside tonight. My mobility is a little slow but I can drive fine. Want me to chauffer you for happy hour? Just say the word.

Without a second thought, Chrissie replied, *Fuck yeah! I need a drink.*

She wasn't sure where to go. Someplace that wouldn't destroy her budget and had a lot of fun, free-spirited energy.

Her mind went to thoughts of old-school drinks and Caribbean steak. *Perfect.*

At home she took a power nap to recuperate from the stress of the morning's events. When she woke up, a fun flirty red dress called out to her. She had much to celebrate. Being healthy and alive was enough, but her celebratory mood was palpable. It was as if she'd searched for meaning and gratitude her whole life and it had suddenly dawned on her like the morning sun. She was learning that emotions of all sorts would come and go, but her gratitude for being alive would always remain. *What a cliché ripe for a social media meme!* she thought and laughed, twirling about her bedroom in her red dress. These moments of joy—so rare in her memory up until recently—made her thankful and look forward to new experiences. She had more hope and expectations for good things than ever before.

She sent Moof a text with the plan. *So old school bar called Oldfields with impeccable quality and Chicago mob era ambiance. Oh, and happy hour prices from five to six p.m. Then, a surprise right down the street with delicious food I think you'll like and fun music.*

Moof replied, *Sounds like a plan. Can I bring my friend Cheryl? She lives nearby and I think you'll get along well.*

Chrissie hesitated slightly. What did she have to lose meeting someone new? She could always get a separate check so she wasn't stuck with someone else's tab.

Yeah that's fine. See you soon.

She put on cute platform sandals. They made her taller without hurting her forty-year-old feet. Then she poured herself a small glass of rosé wine as an appetizer while she sat on the couch, nervously waiting for her pickup like a teen girl on prom night.

Finally, her phone pinged. Moof was here.

She locked the door and checked it twice. Then she walked down the steps to her masterful carriage that awaited—Moof's old minivan with peeling paint.

Inside, a jovial brunette with Bettie Page bangs smiled widely at Chrissie. She wore huge red acrylic hoop earrings with dangling palm trees and her lips were as red as can be.

"Hi, Chrissie. Nice to meet you!"

"Hi, Cheryl." She was quickly surprised as Cheryl gave her a warm hug and a compliment about her dress.

Chrissie sized her up on the spot. This would be *fun*. Chrissie directed Moof on how to get to Oldfields Bar. Upon arriving, he parked next to the entrance and grabbed his cane. He moved slowly, like a cautious elephant, and stopped at the first table he came to, plopping himself down. Sweating a bit and breathing heavily, Chrissie noticed Moof did not look well. She wondered if he was suffering more than he wanted to share.

Before she went to the bar, she checked on him. "Do you want an Old Grand-Dad if they have it?"

He coughed before laughing. "A-ha! No thanks, just Diet Coke for me tonight. Want to drive you lovely ladies home tonight safely."

Chrissie smiled at his charm, but inside she was beginning to worry about him.

Cheryl was already at the bar flirting with the bartender. She and Chrissie both ordered the Oldfields Hemingway, a delicious take on the classic, with rye whiskey instead of rum, beautifully served in a coupe glass. They took their drinks and a Diet Coke over to the table where Moof sat, where he was dabbing his sweaty forehead with a handkerchief he kept in his coat pocket.

He forced a smile.

"Cheers!" You could tell Cheryl needed a night out. She moved with the energy of a newly freed woman.

"I'm celebrating getting divorced!" Cheryl said. "It was a long road, but I'm no longer being physically abused by my high school 'sweetheart.'" She threw her fingers up in air quotations around that odd nickname. "And I am *so* ready for a new chapter in my life."

"Cheers to that," Chrissie added, and clinked her glass in solidarity.

"I finally have a good job, and my own apartment. My daughter is off to college. Now I can focus on myself and being healthy." Chrissie could tell Cheryl was in the mood to share. She continued, "I remember the last straw for me. It had gotten bad before, but something inside me had changed. I had just finished cooking dinner after a full day at work. He kept insulting me. Saying my cooking was horrible. And then he hit me with a pan that was still warm and I slumped on the kitchen floor. He hit me again and left a burn that scarred my arm permanently." She rolled up her dress sleeve to expose a mangled slab of flesh and scar tissue.

Chrissie gasped.

"Then it was like an angel came to help me and give me strength. The angel felt like a warm presence in my heart who told me I didn't deserve this. And I pulled myself up off that floor and took a rolling pin and *smacked his fucking head with it over and over again.* When the police came they took him away in handcuffs. He knew who couldn't hide anymore. They had so much history already about our fights." Cheryl shook her head. "I remember once in group therapy, someone said the police can only do so much. It's in our hearts that we decide we are worth more, that we set boundaries and change our lives. And then my daughter and I moved away. I got a restraining order and took my life back. Sometimes I feel embarrassed that it took me so long to say enough was enough. But my daughter reminds me every day that I'm blessed, I'm still alive—*and* I'm hot. She tells me, 'Mama, you're hot so don't think life has passed you by. Everybody loves you.'"

Chrissie's eyes had welled up with tears and laughter as she cheered on Cheryl. She had so much to be grateful for. Yes, the abuse from her mom and boss was harsh and hurtful, but this woman had endured physical suffering and degradation for years. Chrissie reached in for a hug. "Congratulations. You *are* lovely. I know you don't know me, but I'm proud of you. I just laid down the law with my mother and filed a complaint with my boss. For too long I thought abuse had to be my everyday life. But finally, I'm awake. I'm done being a punching bag for other people. We deserve *more*."

Moof sat there silently, sipping his Diet Coke, an approving smirk peeking out underneath his mustache.

Ready for dinner, they closed out their bar tab and helped Moof walk out to the car. His legs seemed to support most of his weight—he just needed a little help to go all the way.

Chrissie felt ominous things were ahead for him. She didn't mean to compare, but it made her life appear so much brighter.

Back in the van, she guided them down the street. They were close enough to walk, but they drove for Moof's sake.

When they turned into the Bamboo parking lot, Chrissie nodded to Cheryl. "Moof, let her get you to a table. I'll park the van."

He didn't argue because he had no choice. Cheryl came around the side of the van and held his arm firmly as he got out, then escorted him to the table almost effortlessly, even while wearing platform heels. Chrissie parked the van and locked it.

Chrissie met her buddies inside. "The Cancun steak is one of the best NY strip steaks you'll ever have. Trust me."

Moof continued with Diet Coke while Cheryl and Chrissie both ordered a caipirinha. Tropical island music played in the background, and Chrissie found herself swaying back and forth in her chair. They started with the jumbo prawn appetizer, which Moof practically swooned over. This was followed by three orders of the Cancun steak. Smothered in a rich sauce and covered in onions, flanked with plantains, black beans, and rice, it all went down so smoothly. Of course, the drinks helped.

Another round of drinks to aid digestion and their table was all smiles. Chrissie really appreciated Cheryl's energy. It was amazing how you really never knew what someone had been through unless they told you. Cheryl was vivacious and joyful and full of life. If some jerk had beaten her, Chrissie wasn't sure she'd still be so filled with *joie de vivre*. She admired Cheryl's strength. She wanted to bottle her joy. She was grateful Moof had invited them out together—and that Chrissie had broken through her own resistance and given them a chance.

Her life was opening up in new ways she had never dreamed of. There was so much possibility. She did not want to squander it.

Chrissie returned from a trip to the ladies' room to find that Moof had taken care of the entire tab. The ladies smothered him with gratitude, which made his cheeks redden. The smile on his face made it all worthwhile.

Chrissie brought the car down to the restaurant-side entrance so they could get Moof easily into the driver's seat. They dropped Chrissie off at her apartment and before getting out, she took down Cheryl's phone number so they could stay in touch. Then Chrissie gently patted Moof's hand. "Hey. Old Grand-Dad. Take care of yourself. Keep me posted on your situation."

He nodded, slightly embarrassed of having to acknowledge the elephant in the room. Diabetic neuropathy with ailing movement was something Chrissie wouldn't wish on her worst enemy. She knew it could not be easily reversed.

Still, that could not stop her thankfulness for such a joy-filled evening. Her anxious trip to the office early this morning seemed a long-distant memory.

She walked up to her apartment, let herself inside, and sat on the couch in awe of how life could surprise you. She kicked off her shoes and lay there easily, not worried about bedtime. Or anything, really. The very cells of her body buzzed with the excitement of real connection.

Her heart was full.

Chrissie awoke to another day of glorious life. She sat at the kitchen table and painted something new. She looked at the picture of her father. "Hey, Giovanni. Thanks for keeping me company."

She swore she could feel his spirit there sometimes—a thoughtful tap, or an unexpected breeze would remind her that he was always with her.

Florence called occasionally, but Chrissie made a point to give herself plenty of time to decide if she wanted to respond or not. She remembered that adhering to her own needs and sticking to her boundaries was key. Everything involving Flo was artificially urgent and critical, dramatized to gain attention. Instead, she asked herself what she wanted at that moment.

Chrissie had finally become wise to Flo's game. She could love her mother *and* not actively participate in that game anymore. She had a right to decide when drama was something she would allow into her life.

With study she was learning that drama was something she had previously invited into her life to feel alive, and because it felt familiar—yet it had done the opposite, leaving her feeling empty and used. *Sometimes, a peaceful and quiet existence painting canvases in your dining room while communing with your dead father is a quite lovely way to spend your time*, Chrissie mused to the stroke of her brush. She continued to train herself—like building muscle memory until an action became automatic—to adopt peace as the standard, to find her joy in peacefulness.

Everything was a process. That included gratitude.

7: EPILOGUE

Growing up, Chrissie often heard people utter the phrase, "The more things change, the more they stay the same." As she healed, she came to guess that those people hadn't experienced the power of energy healing and attentive self-study and awareness.

Over time, Chrissie learned to perform her own past-life regressions and self-analysis, tapping into professional help when she felt blind spots arise or the need for an independent party's input. But she didn't accept help blindly. She always made sure their input resonated with her own truth. She no longer groveled at the altar of other people's superiority. She finally learned that everyone was human, and she had to be the foremost authority in her own life.

She'd completed twenty-two paintings—enough to create a twenty-two-card tarot deck. As it turned out, Avril knew someone in Eagle Rock who'd developed their own tarot card set and was happy to share some of their knowledge with Chrissie.

Marcus, Shilling, and Rosenbaum had taken an unexpected twist. Vanessa Kriper had been let go for unprofessional behavior and violation of the company's code of ethics. Chrissie was offered the opportunity to work under a new leader, Mr. Spencer, who'd been noticed for his ability to encourage and inspire new talent—quite the opposite of The Griper. Chrissie had felt like old talent at her age, but Mr. Spencer encouraged her to take a business strategy class and welcomed her unconventional perspective at meetings.

Chrissie was learning that as she changed, the situations around her could adapt in unexpected ways. It was like walking through a door into a parallel universe where all the things she never imagined could happen were possible.

Having a stable position at work with positive reinforcement helped Chrissie build her self-esteem. She finally vowed to take real vacation time every year instead of putzing around or whining about not having enough money or friends to join her. She took a long weekend trip to California's Santa Ynez wine country and was pleasantly joined by her new friend, Cheryl. Chrissie had been willing to do the trip solo, but had been blessed with a lovely companion who gave her the right amount of alone time and the perfect companionship when desired.

So it was that Chrissie sat at a vineyard, watching the hills roll on serenely for miles while the wind blew through her hair.

Her phone rang with a call from Moof, who was checking in on their trip. Since their lovely adventure months ago, he'd had his right leg amputated beneath the knee. His foot had developed gangrene—it had been the only way to save his leg, and his life.

He spent most of his time in a subpar facility in the valley covered by Medicare. It was better than being homeless, yet still a sad place to visit, filled with doubled-up rooms and few amenities. One bright spot nearby was a Thai restaurant a block down the street. Chrissie would meet Moof's wife at the facility, where they would take turns pushing him in his wheelchair down the street. Medicare had yet to approve an electric wheelchair. His wife fondly said they'd soon give Moof the "electric chair"—that always got a hearty "A-ha!" out of

Moof. At 295 pounds, pushing his wheelchair down paved valley sidewalks was no joke. Chrissie liked to think his positive energy helped grease the wheels and move him along a little more easily.

At the Thai restaurant, they'd share a big bowl of spicy Tom Yum shrimp soup, plus some fried rice. Then they'd take turns wheeling him back to the facility where he'd lay alone in a bed, staring at the ceiling for hours.

Chrissie answered the phone, her hello coming out slowly thanks to the wine.

"Hey, kiddo. How are you gals doing?"

"We're having a great time here. Wish you could join us. I'll send you a photo of the lovely hills and some of our favorite wines so far. I'm... really sorry you can't be here."

"A-ha! You're sweet. Don't worry about it, kiddo. Focus on yourself. Don't make the same mistakes I made."

"What do you mean?"

"Remember that one time when you asked me why I listen to other people so well?"

"Yeah?"

"Well, I thought I was going to be a priest... and I *am* good at listening. But... long ago, focusing on other people became a way to avoid facing myself."

Chrissie felt horrible right then, like she'd used him, even though he'd given himself away freely.

Moof continued, "I was so afraid of therapy. That if they dug in and I started to let go and share, my pain would never end. Like Pandora's Box. And now I have nothing but time to face myself."

"I'm sorry, Moof."

"Don't waste your energy with that, kiddo. Live your life. Continue to show me every day how you reinvent yourself. You give me hope."

"Thanks," she said softly. "I have a short deck of five sample cards with me from my new tarot deck. Can I pull a card for you?"

"A-ha! Sure."

"For now, I've titled them 'Spark Your Inner Genius Cards.' You know... reminding people to trust their own inner wisdom."

"I like that! Sounds promising."

Chrissie said a quick prayer over the deck, then cut the short stack of cards, revealing Moof's guidance. "So no joke... your card is 'Reinvention and Healing.' The image on the card is a fun play on the traditional 'Hanged Man' tarot card. It pictures a woman hanging upside down from a tree with a glass of wine right-side-up in one hand and a selenite wand in the other."

"Hey, I remember that! You showed me a photo of that painting!"

Chrissie smiled. "Yeah, that's right. The tree branch is about to break, but the woman is laughing like a hysterical hyena, unaware of what is about to transpire. I'll read the guidance on the card to you. 'Healing is crazy, right? You go inward to face one trauma about yourself and the whole ball of yarn unravels. It's like your life is the yarn and the divine is the cat. It's fucking with you and having a grand ole time in the process. Healing and reinvention are two sides of the same coin. As you shed old stuff—baggage—you see things differently. You make different choices. Sometimes life rearranges itself on your behalf. It's almost always scary when life shifts. In this case, it's like the Rumi quote: "Do not worry that your life is turning upside down. How do you know the side you are used to is better than the one to come?" Sometimes it feels worse before it feels better. There is no easy fix. You are not alone, and you are not doing anything wrong.'"

The other end of the line was silent for a time. Chrissie thought she heard sniffling. Finally Moof said, "That is lovely. It definitely gives this old man food for thought. When are you going to officially launch these cards?"

"Maybe later this year. I'm not in a rush right now. The act of creating this has me

feeling so good about myself. It's like I finally mattered enough to myself to follow my heart."

"Good on you. I'm so proud of you, kiddo. So what comes next?"

"Thanks. For now, I'm going to focus on my next glass of wine."

I hope you enjoyed this book. If so, it would really help me if you left a review online. Thank you for your support!

HeatherMartinAuthor.com